Malcom C. Salaman

Woman - Through a Man's Eyeglass

Malcom C. Salaman

Woman - Through a Man's Eyeglass

ISBN/EAN: 9783744755320

Printed in Europe, USA, Canada, Australia, Japan

Cover: Foto ©Andreas Hilbeck / pixelio.de

More available books at **www.hansebooks.com**

WOMAN—THROUGH A MAN'S EYE-GLASS

Woman—Through a Man's Eyeglass

BY MALCOLM C. SALAMAN

WITH ILLUSTRATIONS

BY DUDLEY HARDY

NEW YORK, 1892 PUBLISHED BY

LOVELL, CORYELL & COMPANY

43, 45 AND 47 EAST TENTH STREET

To

HER WHO FIRST TAUGHT ME THE

LOVABLENESS OF WOMAN

MY MOTHER

Several of these Ladies were informally and appropriately presented by the "Gentlewoman." In somewhat new attire, however, they make their reappearance, joined by my Lady Fin-de-Siècle.

CONTENTS

WOMAN—

THROUGH A MAN'S EYEGLASS

PREAMBLE

WITHOUT womam man is nought; and the proverb, *Cherchez la femme*, though commonly urged with a cynical sneer, is as full of humane wisdom as any saying of Solomon.

When I contemplate woman in the abstract, with all her divine gentleness and sympathy, and her essential spirituality, I feel that I must kneel and worship her from afar; but when I regard her in the concrete, with all those little weaknesses and vanities and sleight-of-mind tricks, which are as the electric wires through which man is brought into familiar and continuous communion with her then I feel that she is near to me, that we can meet on a common plane of humanity, and that the privilege of loving her is not beyond my reach. And to love woman is surely the highest privilege of life, and the noblest duty.

It is but a shallow philosophy that underrates the married state, and he who bids you avoid matrimony, because he has tried it and failed, is a fool for his pains and deserved his fate, for he chose rashly and without discrimination. "Wife and children," as Bacon says, "are a kind of discipline of humanity." Your true philosopher will tell you that the enduring companionship of a good woman is the most beautiful influence in a man's life, but it must be hoped for only after an ample apprenticeship in love, through which alone a man can arrive at any true knowledge of woman. Your wise man will never marry his first love, for he knows that matrimony demands as much special education as any of the learned professions. Yet the number of unqualified amateurs who enter the matrimonial ranks every year is perfectly appalling to contemplate, the Divorce Court annals recording but an infinitesimal portion of the spoiled lives for which the lack of conjugal education is responsible. And yet I am not inclined to set much store by the wisdom of Thales, who, when asked, as one of the Seven Wise Men of Greece, to prescribe the proper period for a man to marry, replied, "A young man not yet; an elder man, not at all." I only feel convinced that incompatibility of temper with Mrs. Thales was at the root of his wisdom, and gave it a false twist.

Does every man of us indeed deserve a wife? or rather, have we all studied to understand a woman and to love her with comprehension? This is not such an easy matter as we think, for when do we know exactly how much of her love a woman expects to give for how much of ours? When can we tell in what proportions she wants us to be severally husband, lover and friend? For if we would maintain that illusion which alone preserves real matrimonial happiness, we must never allow the relations of lover and companion to appear lost in that of husband. The essence of woman is in her love, the substance remains for domesticity; and when the happy state of marriage proves a failure, be sure that there has been misconception as to the relativeness of the one and the other. After I shall have written that great work I have in contemplation, to be entitled "The Wooing of Women:

by a Practical Failure," there shall be no more unhappy marriages ; for my readers will then learn to recognise the adaptable wife and avoid the unsuitable, and the wooing shall be conducted on such scientific principles that all misunderstandings will be rectified in the probationary stage, and a matrimonial millennium will set in. Then, perchance, the writers of romance may look in vain to real life for their plots ; but a grateful posterity will write my epitaph, " He made true love run smooth."

But you may ask, why have *I* never married ? Well, the answer is a long story in many chapters ; but perhaps I may summarise it in a sentence. I have always loved too much. This statement will, no doubt, be regarded as a confession of frequent infidelity, and perhaps I may be misconstrued as a kind of gay Lothario. But I am really no such thing. Though the names of my loves have been many, I have—paradoxical as it may sound—loved the same woman all my life. She is only a fantasy of the heart ; yet I have sometimes thought that, after much seeking, I had found the original in flesh and blood, and I have invested her with all the attributes of the ideal woman, the wife of my dreaming, the complement of myself.

Then I have loved to idolatry, turned life into a perpetual love-making, and suffered tortures of jealousy until the real woman has revealed herself behind the image of the ideal, and proved but another case of mistaken identity.

Yet, though I were less than human, did I not feel some sort of sorrow or disappointment at the first perception of my mistake, it has left no bitterness, for the fault has been invariably my own. I had clothed with my own ideas an entity sufficiently beautiful in herself, and loved her, not for the woman that she was, but for the woman that I wanted her to be. How, then, could there be perfect sympathy between us? We were playing at cross-purposes. If she cared for me at all, it was as one who loved her for herself; not as one who was endeavouring to model her to the mould of his own mind, when he found that, after all, she was a misfit. The misunderstanding was of my own making for, as I am beginning to find out, ideals are impracticable in the commerce of life. To be happy, one must have no preconceived notions, but "catch the joy as it flies," and accept that which is for what it is.

Nevertheless, though my life has been a series of individual disillusionings, and while I cannot but feel that

an excellent husband has been squandered in me, I
have never loved in vain.   Even in my sorrowful
awakenings to the fact that the One Woman is still a
Will-o'-the-Wisp to me, and that she whom I had permitted to personate her, and had taken to my heart in
her place, is, after all, hopelessly separate from me, I
have invariably felt the better for the experience.   Our
natures always gain by love, even though it be fruitless; it opens the pores of our souls, and lets in
charity, which is the very sap of society.   And each
fresh experience of love adds to one's store of sympathy, and increases one's knowledge of "Womanity"
—if I may be allowed the term—and consequently
one's power of loving.   "Appetite grows by what it
feeds on," and so the more one loves the more one
needs to love, and it is very pleasant.

Who that has suffered much from love of woman
would not willingly pay double the price in heart-aches
to buy back "love's young dream?"   For my own
part, I would sooner be miserable in love than happy
out of it; but then there are those with whom to love
is as necessary as to breathe.   I am not ashamed to
confess it is so with me, for is not love the most beautiful element in life?   Nor have I any sympathy with

those cynical minded persons who regard absolute
devotion to a woman as feebly foolish. Though
bachelorhood has become almost chronic with me, I
still never meet a woman without wondering whether
she and I could love each other under appropriate
circumstances. And surely it is this capacity to give
and take in the matter of the affections that preserves
our youth for us; while we retain it, we can never
grow old, though our years may increase apace. When
we feel that we are open to no new sensations of love,
then let us prepare for old age, and turn an indifferent
ear to the sound of funeral bells. But while one can
say, "What a charming woman; I believe I could
love her," one feels that life is still worth living, and
full of beautiful possibilities.

It has been a fashion in all ages to decry women, to
call them false and fickle, to say that their business is
to deceive, that their spell is that of the serpent, that
they are vain and shallow and cruel. Poets have railed
against them in plausible verse; philosophers have
said bitter things about them; and many a wit has
gained his reputation at the expense of woman's fame;
all of which is as wickedly foolish as to say that human
nature is uniformly infamous. You will not find that

the great writers who live in the hearts of mankind ever stultified or debased their genius by defaming woman ; but, on the contrary, they have created for us immortal types of pure and lovely womanhood. It is the cheapest cynicism to discredit a whole sex ; and misogyny and misanthropy are merely the affectations of vain and egotistical minds. When I hear a man say he does not believe in woman's constancy or woman's virtue, I know that there is something wrong with that man : he is either a libertine or a bully, and no woman will ever respect him, however much he may ensnare her senses.

Belief in woman must be part of the religion of all men who are worthy of their mothers. By this I do not mean that one must take for gospel her every word and act, for the gift of dissimulation is a special dispensation of Nature for her protection against what is aggressive or destructive in man ; just as to the female of the African butterfly *Papilio merope* is accorded the power of protecting herself, during certain seasons, against the depredations of birds, by assuming the colour of the malodorous *Amauris niavius*, which is particularly obnoxious to the feathered tribes. And as we recognise the humour of this comedy of the mimic butterfly and the cunningly duped bird, so do we perceive, if we be true critics of the stage of life, that nine-tenths of its comedy are due to the protective dissimulation of woman in her relations with man. Else were it all drama, with an excess of tragedy, and that were dreary. Woman is full of quaint conceit and subtle humour, whether she know it herself or not, and we love her all the more for this, especially since the laugh is often against ourselves.

Confidence between man and woman must always be comparative, and absolute trust a practicable impossibility, since the differences of temperament preclude a perfect understanding. A man can never see a woman entirely as she is, or as one of her own sex may see her, and *vice versâ*. Yet a woman is more likely to comprehend a man and his motives than he is to comprehend her; for a woman, while more sensitively sympathetic, judges instantly by instinct, straight and sure as the crow flies. A man, on the other hand, travels the railroad of reason, where there are many shuntings, and a single mistaken signal may upset the whole train of his logic. In judging a woman's motives and feelings a man argues from his own, and deduces conclusions which are, more often than not, radically erroneous.

For instance, a man kisses the woman he loves, and she responds to his caress. He believes it is in the same passionate spirit, but really the impulse is subtly different. He kisses her to satisfy his own yearning; she kisses him because she knows it will make him happy, and to make him happy is the active spirit of her love. And it is just the failure of man to distinguish and accept this beautiful spirituality in woman's relations with him, which necessitates that protective dissimulation which becomes her second nature. For example, here the woman must simulate the passion of her lover, for he would not be satisfied with the delicate impulse of her responsive caress; so is he permitted to believe that she feels as he does, reasoning only from his own emotions, while she instinctively knows that their feelings are running in different channels, though they meet in the broad ocean of love. How true to womanhood is that passage in the journal of that extraordinary girl, Marie Bashkirtseff, where, relating how, in response to the passionate protestations of a youthful lover, she kissed him, she adds, "I did it more for his sake than mine." Did the young man think it was for his sake? Not a bit of it. He thought it was a passionate impulse for her own gratification, as any man in his place would have thought.

But what must be the result of all this misunderstanding if the lover be one of your unqualified amateurs? After marriage the wife, happy in the possession of the husband she loves, believes that all is mutual trust, and she ceases to practise that beautifully innocent dissimulation by which she held him as a lover. Then he begins to misunderstand, and her love seems not the same to him, though it has been unchanged all the while; so his love grows colder as he becomes consequently dissatisfied and irritable, and, with this rift within the lute, the music of matrimony sounds out of tune and grates upon their ears, and the lovers drift into mere husband and housewife — lovers no more.

But I am getting serious and psychological, and what has an incorrigible bachelor like me to do with the psychology of woman? I have but to glance round my companionless room, and a photograph on the mantelpiece, a picture on the wall, a book on the shelf, a faded letter-case on the table, will remind me how little I really know of it all; else, perhaps, who knows? the wife of my dreams might even now be sitting in that chair yonder, where those books and newspapers rest in such confusion, and the sweet, happy voices of children might be waking the slumbering soul of the room to joyous laughter, and I should not want an excuse to fling away my pen, and romp on the floor with the little ones, and play with their toys, while *she* smiled happily, and called me a "great baby."

No; let me believe that I know nothing of woman now, as I knew nothing then—how long ago? Is it years, months, weeks, days—what matter? Regret is for the failures of marriage, and time a matter for the Benedicts. I can dream a whole life's happiness between waking and bedtime, and choose my bride from any age or clime I will. Helen of Troy or Guinevere of Camelot shall be she if I dream it so, and I'll snap my fingers at Paris or Lancelot, and yet remain a free man, with an undisputed smile for the young lady who sells me my morning paper. So let me be a dreamer still, and woman a beautiful fantasy.

But some memories are pleasant, so if you, my reader, care to listen, as we sit together in the hush of the twilight, I will sketch you portraits of some typical women I have known—not necessarily loved ; and if I chance to dip my brush in cynicism, I pray you stop me, for I would not be a caricaturist, but if I happen to lay the tint of tenderness on my canvas a little too thickly, forgive it, since the subject is a woman

THE LITTLE WIDOW

A LITTLE widow is a dangerous thing; but is there not always a fascination in dangerous things? A little learning, for instance, gives a sparkling flavour to life, whereas much learning oppresses it. Now a little widow is perilously fascinating, as a great, tall widow rarely is; her very littleness constitutes an element of danger, since it coaxingly compels sympathy, and when one sympathises with a widow, when one says "Poor little woman!"—one is lost. Though one may not marry her, one is nevertheless her slave. Little Mrs. Willoweed is the most irresistible woman I ever met. I defy any man not to fall in love with her, be it for a day, a week, a year; and it must be always a sudden fall. He is heart-whole one day, and desperately in love the next. It is magnetic and mysterious.

When it happened to me, for the life of me I could

not tell how it came about, or why I was in love. I only knew there was a kind of spell in the atmosphere. We were together up the river, the afternoon tea-basket had done its duty, the rest of our party had scattered in different directions, and Mrs. Willoweed and I had wandered into a cornfield, where we discussed Shelley and plucked poppies in the soft sunny haze of an August afternoon. Whether it was the passionate suggestiveness of the poppies, or whether it was the influence of "Epipsychidion," I know not; but it seemed to me on a sudden that Mrs. Willoweed was the only being worth living for, and, as our hands were drawn by some mysterious impulse to the same poppy, I took her hand instead of the flower and held it. She did not take it away, but let it rest in mine almost caressingly, while she said, with a bewitchingly mischievous smile "Isn't this a little ridiculous?" The incongruity of the remark and the action completely captured me. What could I do but justify my impulse with a declaration of love? She listened with a pretty, feigned surprise, and said exactly the things which experience no doubt had taught her would drive her victory home. You see she was a little widow, and was consequently a complete compendium of the art of love. That is why little widows are so dangerous. They not only know their own sex, but they know ours too, and knowledge is power.

Of course I wanted to marry Mrs. Willoweed, because she declared she would never marry again; and day after day I would exercise all my persuasive ingenuity in arguing her into a matrimonial frame of mind. But she was obdurate; a second husband presented no attraction to her. She had tasted the sweets of wedded life, she knew all about conjugal bliss, but somehow single blessedness, decked in the latest *mode* of widow's weeds, offered her a more alluring programme than a revival of the marriage vows. So, although she accepted my devotion along with the rest, she persisted in saying me nay; but she said it in such a fascinating manner that I was never tired of listening to it. She would always veil her "No!" with a delicate gauzy suggestion of "Yes!" She would keep a distant chance of an affirmative hovering in the air, as it were, and I consequently never broached the subject without that sort of sensation which a gambler experiences at a roulette table, or that which excited the members of the Suicide Club when the president used to deal the fateful cards;

and while she kept me hovering on the brink
of matrimony she would play upon my affections
with the most exquisite science. She would
assert her positive incapacity to be constant, which
to a man of sentiment and spirit, as I trust I am,
was of course a positive chal-
lenge to prove
her otherwise.
Constancy has
always

been one of woman's proud-
est boasts, whether truthfully
or not is a question of individual experience, and
therefore for a woman to urge her probable inconstancy as an excuse for not marrying a man who asked
her, was only to make him more ardent in his suit.
Then, again Mrs. Willoweed would tell me quite

frankly that to be engaged to me would make her uninteresting in the eyes of all her other male acquaintances, while her women friends would cease to be jealous of her. Perhaps this latter reason was not very complimentary to me, but it had the intended effect, it made me still more demonstrative in my devotion.

Little Mrs. Willoweed has the science of flirtation at her finger-tips, she has reduced the teasing of hearts to a mathematical system, and she sets herself problems merely for the pleasure of solving them, and judging the effect upon her own vanity. Her flirtation is as different from that of the *ingénue*, or the experienced spinster, or even the flighty married woman, as a complex algebraical equation is from a simple rule-of-three sum. With all the experience of married life she has the sense of perfect freedom and irresponsibility ; consequently her flights in flirtation are as daring as they are without fear or reproach.

But let it not be thought that Mrs. Willoweed has ever flown defiantly into the face of Mrs. Grundy, though that estimable lady keeps her hawk-eyes wide open and constantly fixed upon Mrs. Willoweed's movements. Naturally the unfettered and unchaperoned conditions of her life invite gossip, but nobody has

ever been able to say a word against her morality.
They certainly whisper, here and there, that a little
more circumspection might be advisable, but then
whose life would be worth living encased in cast-iron
conventionalities and pinioned by prudery? Mrs.
Willoweed enjoys her life, she revels in her freedom,
and captures as many heart-slaves as she can ; but she
never trips. She can always look society in the face
without a blush, she can always laugh in the face of
propriety without offence.

Though I no longer want to marry Mrs. Willoweed,
having lived to learn all her little ways through watching her practise her experiments on those others
whom I had once thought my rivals, I will yet yield to
none in my admiration for her, and I am prepared to
champion her through thick and thin. She is a delightful litt'e creature, and it is not her fault if men
will fall in love with her ; she only helps them to do
it pleasantly. And there is a great charm in loving
a woman who is versed in the lore of love, and who
is practised in all the sleight-of-heart tricks of it. The
woman who merely subjects herself to a man's love,
and adds no fresh fuel from her own sentimental
activity, soon wearies him so that the flame dies out ;

but the woman who employs her arts in feeding the love of a man, who knows by instinct and experience when to tease and when to coax, when to starve and when to feast, may keep that love as long as she cares to.

This is the secret of Mrs. Willoweed's supremacy. She knows all this, and never makes a mistake. This is how she keeps so many of her old admirers. Life is to her a game of cards, in which hearts are always trumps; and she plays the game so prettily that, even though she never loses, there is never a whisper of unfairness. Perhaps if she were a little more cautious not to let outsiders see so much of the game, it would be none the worse for her; but, with all her skill at heart-conjuring, she is a very guileless little person.

Her own heart is open as the day to melting sympathy, and she is as innocent as daylight. She never hides anything, she never does anything to hide; she only tries to live cheerily and pleasantly, and make as many people happy as possible. Why should she be condemned to wear moral sackcloth and ashes all her life because she is a widow and does not choose to marry again? She does not concern herself about

the goings-on of other women.; why should they be
so anxious to catch her tripping, why should they
be always on the watch? Of course she never means
to give them the chance, but, nevertheless, it is irk-
some to feel that every woman's eye is open against
her, every woman's ear ready to catch the faintest
suggestion of an echo of a rumour. Why is it?

Surely it is not because Mrs. Willoweed is exceedingly
pretty and remarkably accomplished, for other women
have been equally so, and yet have failed to awaken
the suspicions of their sex and to keep Mrs. Grundy on
the *qui vive*. It cannot be because Mrs. Willoweed
dresses so beautifully, that, whether in walking costume, tea-gown, or ball-dress, she looks as though the
art of attire has reached on her its climax of perfection, for there be as good dresses in Bond Street
as ever came out of it, and all beautiful women are
made to be well-dressed Mrs. Willoweed has no
monopoly.

Mrs. Willoweed is a pretty little widow, and there
is the gist of the matter. Like Hester Prynne, she
carries about her a scarlet letter, though visible only
to the mental eye of women with husbands and
brothers and lovers, and that letter is D, which stands

for Dangerous. You see there is no barrier of in-
genuousness to be broken down, no safeguard of a
husband-in-law. She is experienced, accessible, and
free, and withal fatally fascinating. She is a dead shot
with Cupid's arrow, and never misses her mark. It is
not, therefore, to be wondered that women with susceptible male belongings fear to trust them within the
magic sphere of Mrs. Willoweed, and that their fears
are apt to get the better of their reason and their
charity. But, after all, poor little Mrs. Willoweed is
entirely innocent of the matrimonial or amorous
designs that are placed to her charge in such a sweeping and illogical fashion.

She has a handsome competence of her own, and
therefore has no mercenary motives for marriage ; and,
indeed, she has no intention of binding any man to
her for life—she always puts it that way, as it sounds
kinder and more philanthropic—but really she has no
desire to part with her liberty again. She is very
happy as she is.

She cannot live without lovers, but she never lets
them get out of their depth, she always keeps them in
check, so that she can pull them back into the safer
waters of friendship whenever she will. Some women

cannot have a man friend without wishing him to be a lover, and when he is a lover, wishing him to be a friend again. Mrs. Willoweed is one of these. Like this grand little kingdom of ours, she has a passion for conquest and empire, but, once the conquest is assured, the annexation completed, and the excitement of the contest over, she sets herself to the task of establishing friendly relations of an enduring character. That is why you never hear a man say an unkind or severe thing about Mrs. Willoweed, dainty, delightful butterfly though she be.

She never quarrels with her admirers, but makes them all feel that it is a privilege to love her, and when we can feel that about a woman, we may be sure there is a great deal of good in her, and we need not be surprised to find there is more chivalrous feeling in us than we gave ourselves credit for. Truly, an innocently frank flirt, like Mrs. Willoweed, can open the valves of a man's heart, and purge it of much unhealthy sentimentality.

Mrs. Willoweed enjoys existence. She lives in an atmosphere of prettiness and lightness, and treads a rosy path with almost winged feet. Wherever she goes she casts her spell of fascination, and she is

always the centre of the pleasantest group. Where
she is, there will gather the brave, the gallant, the
witty, and, where these are, beauty is drawn as by
magnetic attraction, however jealous it may be of the
original magnet—the little widow. Haughty beauty
may sneer, and Mrs. Grundy may put on her spec-
tacles, and gather her skirts close, but little Mrs.
Willoweed—bright, innocent, playful little Mrs. Willoweed—is the queen of the hour. All the men love
her, and "she is such fun."

See her dispensing afternoon tea in her own dainty
drawing-room, with its bizarre Orientalism suggesting
the boudoir of some Eastern princess in the "Arabian
Nights"; she is clad in a picturesque tea-gown, which
is itself quite a poem in drapery, while her graceful
movements are its rhythm. Can you wonder at that
group of admirers sitting around her, each seeming
most anxious for the departure of the others? It is a
pleasant spell to be under; I would not be out of
its reach for worlds. Why, Mrs. Willoweed's busy
talk is a mental tonic, and her laugh is as exhilarating
as sparkling wine. To drink tea with her *tête-à-tête* of
an afternoon is a delightful privilege; and there is
always the added excitement of fearing the intrusion

of other visitors. Unfortunately, there are always so many candidates for this pleasure.

You see, Mrs. Willoweed is not a woman with a mission of any kind; she has plenty of money, plenty of leisure, and nothing to do, and she devotes her life to doing it as delightfully as possible. A little widow may be a dangerous thing, but the danger is harmless; at least, I am sure it is so with little Mrs. Willoweed.

MY MOTHER

THIS is my birthday, and it is not unnatural that I should be thinking of my mother. Let me talk to you of her, for in all the world of women I know of none so near perfection. I say this in no mere boastful spirit. It is my firm conviction, the result of a life's experience; and I say it, moreover, in the full consciousness that there are millions of men ready to challenge my statement in favour of their own mothers. And it is well that it should be so. I am glad to think it, for good mothers, by their very love-worthiness, preserve the moral equilibrium of the world. Therefore, I am happy to believe that other men think their mothers superior to mine though I have the advantage of them, for they do not know mine as I do, in the relation of mother and son. That makes all the difference. To every man worthy of the name his mother must be an

angel of goodness, the object of his holiest devotion.
Why, the very word suggests the most sacred senti-
ments of humanity; it is a beautiful word, and one
that most readily inspires all that is tender and gentle
and pure in feeling. What, for instance, could be
more tender than those lines of Edgar Allan Poe's,
most passionate, intemperate, and truly poetic of
poets?

> " Because I feel that, in the heavens above,
> The angels, whispering to one another,
> Can find among their burning terms of love,
> None so devotional as that of ' mother.' "

But I am not going to dilate upon the merits of
mothers generally. I only want to tell you what
manner o' mother mine is, and how happy I am to be
able to say *is* and not *was*, like so many poor bachelors
of my acquaintance. For a man who is growing old,
with neither wife nor child to bring him loving greetings
on his birthday, I can conceive nothing more awful
than to have no mother who shall say, " Bless you, my
son!" while in so doing she happily remembers, in a
gentle autumn mood of love, all that full flowering
summer love with which she greeted him on that first
birthday of his. In a man's youth, when all the world
is opening before him, with its exuberant growth of

possibilities tempting him in all directions, and when the gaudy butterflies of passion are leading him a chase through brakes and brambles with their deep wounding prickles and nettles that sting, his mother ceases for a time to be the guiding star of his life as she had been in his childhood, for there are so many other lights that flash a-cross his way, and one serves as well as another to illuminate his onward course.   But when he retraces his steps, wounded and weary, and longing for rest, he seeks again the steady starlight of a mother's love.   A man who has known any sorrow or disappointment or disillusioning, turns childlike, by instinct to the repose and the solace of his mother's bosom, where there is always a fount

of love as fresh as in the days when he would come
to her to stop his floods of childish tears with
those caresses that only a mother can give to her
child.

Yes, it is my birthday, and I am happy ; but last
night I was in a melancholy mood, and wandered
aimlessly through green lanes and over a bridge, while
across the moonlit river, which looked so peacefully
beautiful, there came from a riverside house, whose
lights gleaming through the grey leafy curtains of the
willows gave it the appearance of some enchanted
palace, sounds of jovial choruses. And these jarred
upon me, for I was lonely, and I was mourning the
dead years and their buried opportunities. Then
I wandered on till I came to the wall of a grave-
yard, and large trees stood on either side of the
road and darkened my way with their shadows,
and I would not walk onwards, for those black
shadows seemed to me like the ghosts of future
years, and I was alone among them, quite alone. So
I retraced my steps, and the moonlight was over the
churchyard, and I stopped and gazed at the tombs, all
mystic in the moonlight, and they seemed to look at
me so piteously and enviously, for they were the
records of dead lives and dead hopes, and I was

still living, I still had love and hope. Then I looked up into the starry heavens, and they were very sweet, and I fancied the stars were so disposed as to spell the word "mother." And then a pure and gentle joy stole through my soul, and I felt that I was not alone, that though many a mother lay cold and dead in that churchyard, my own dear little mother lived, lived cheerful, happy, and full of love. So last night's melancholy passed away at the thought of her, and to-day I feel in the mood to bless all the world and everything in it that I have a mother, and such a mother, too.

And still, you will say, I have not described her to you. Well, how can a man describe his own mother? She is just—my mother, and that is all I can tell you. That must convey to you a picture of ideal goodness, common sense, and unselfish love—in fact, as I said before, motherhood in perfection.

Somebody told me the other day that a woman cannot possibly devote herself equally to her husband and her children; that one must give way to the other, and she—it was a woman who said this—instanced the cases of several devotedly domestic women of our mutual acquaintance. And, when we came to examine facts, I was bound to admit that she was right in every case she had cited; but this did not convince me that her argument held good invariably. I refuted it at one fell swoop with my mother.

I am absolutely certain that my father—God bless him!—would bear me out in this, after all his forty odd years of wedded life, and I can confidently count upon the confirmatory evidence of my brothers and sisters. Never have we or my father had the slightest reason to be jealous of one another on account of my mother's attention to the other. She has the most marvellous power of dividing her devotion equally between her husband and her children, and this supremely womanly virtue has enabled her always to preserve an equiibrium of happiness between her husband, her children, and herself. It makes me so angry to hear cynics sneering at the possibility of enduring happiness in married life, when I think of my father and mother sitting together in their old age as cheerfully as when the romance of life was still fresh for them, and urging folks to matrimony because it is the happier state. To see him at his piano, pouring out in melodious reverie the emotions that are ever fresh in him, while she sits close by in her armchair, revelling in love stories that would set the hearts of romantic schoolgirls aflame, is, I think, one of the most beautiful sights in the world, and it makes one feel that a burden of seventy or eighty years may be borne lightly and easily if only love be there to keep the heart young.

In childhood one's mother seems always such a distance off in the matter of age, but when one has reached middle life, and the wheels of existence need oiling with the encouragement of affection, one's mother comes nearer, and seems younger and less sophisticated than ourselves. For instance, to-day I feel a kind of Methuselah, and, as I think of my mother and all her little ways, I can scarcely believe that she is so much older than I. I think of her now as she was when we were all children ; I recall the fairy stories she used to tell us to keep us good and quiet, while my father was busily occupied with his music, and quiet was absolutely necessary for him to produce work that satisfied him. So did she maintain a practical sympathy with his pursuits, while she rejoiced our young minds. So has she ever been ; in sickness or in health she has never sacrificed her husband or her children for each other, but considered them equally.

I remember once when I was seriously ill, and my father was taken ill at the same time, how she would spend her whole time equally between the two sick-rooms, yet never allow either to feel the slightest want. Most devoted and skilful of sick nurses, her gentle cheerfulness, her little touches of humour, especially when there is any noxious physic to be swallowed, and her undemonstrative sympathy, make her presence by the invalid couch a sweet restorative in itself. How many weary hours of illness has she solaced for me, from childhood to manhood! One says confidently to the woman one loves that life without her would be empty and unbearable; and it is a beautiful dispensation that the emotion of love can make one feel this. But let the man who has known a mother's devotion through life, imagine what it would mean to be rett of that. *I* dare not, and why should I? My mother is as young a woman for her seventy-five years as you would wish to meet, and as her grandchildren come, she seems to grow younger for her joy of them. For she loves children, and understands them, and she knows how to win their love and make them

c

happy.   I do not believe there was ever so scientifically sympathetic a tender of babies as my mother.
She seems to divine their dumb eloquence, and know
exactly what they feel and want to express.

My mother is brimming over with humanity, and
her indignation is easily aroused by anything approaching to injustice. She cannot sit quietly in a theatre
during the performance of a play wherein children are
ill-treated, but must loudly give vent to her indignation.   If she sees two boys fighting in the street, she
will promptly push her way through the encouraging
crowd, and threaten to "call a policeman " if they do
not desist ; and if she comes across a woman who is
chastising a naughty child, or a man who is correcting
an obstreperous animal, she will not hesitate to stop
and "give it to them well," as she calls the delivering
of a reprimand. She is actively compassionate towards
all suffering, sympathetic with all sorrow, and pity-
ingly tolerant of any error arising from that ignorance
which is the heritage of poverty or the disadvantages
of birth.   But, on the other hand, she is aggressively
intolerant of all cant and its consequences ; she is a
sworn foe to humbug in any shape or form, and

candour is personified in her attitude towards all men and all women.

Occasionally my father will be carried away by that beautiful credulity and enthusiasm which belong to the idealist nature, but my mother's common-sense view of the case will, after some discussion, invariably prove to be the true one. If this result in any disappointment concerning the character of a friend, or the gratitude of a *protégé*, my father will console himself with the reflection that there must always be exceptions, and he will continue to believe in universal goodness and the Providence that watches over it. But my mother will become shrewder in the future, and so her common-sense will act as a brake upon my father's idealism. Not that she is matter of-fact, beyond realising the fact that the world is made to live in, as well as dream in, and that living is an obligation, whilst dreaming is a luxury. With her the *desiderata* of life have always been peace and quiet; and her ideal of pleasure is to live in a cottage in the country, with a rose-covered porch, and a garden in which every imaginable flower, fruit, or vegetable may be cultivated, in which her grandchildren may have ample scope to play and enjoy themselves, and her husband and children may also find joy and comfort. She is never so happy as when in the country, where, freed from the cares of housekeeping, she is able to ramble about with a little grandson or granddaughter for companion, and gather ferns, or tend flowers, or feed birds. These simple pleasures are absolute delights to her; there is no humbug about them, no chance of their disturbing the calm with troublous argument.

How my memory goes back to those days of child-hood, when we would all go to the seaside or to some country place in the summer months, and my mother would speedily become the beloved of the country folk by reason of her simple love of Nature, as well as by her sympathetic interest in their lives of toil, or her skill in suggesting remedies for the rheumatic aged or the ailing young. Wherever my mother has been she has always carried love and gratitude with her. And if this be so among strangers, what must it be with us who have known her love all our lives? Ah, we, her children, have indeed a store of gratitude, which it is the highest, most blessed privilege to feel. It is on a man's birthday that he pauses to think of all this; to calculate the amount of love that is his, and

the amount of love and gratitude that he gives in
return, and when he can include a living mother's love
in the balance, he is blessed indeed. That is why I
feel so happy to-day ; my mother greets me, and you
know that she is the sweetest, the —well, she is my
mother, God bless her !

THE SOCIALLY AMBITIOUS WOMAN

ALTHOUGH there is little or nothing about Mrs. Vere Veneer that connoisseurs would mistake for Vere de Vere, to the casual observer and the Society "outsider" she presents quite an imposing appearance from the social point of view. Whenever she is present at any social function, the "Society papers" duly chronicle the gown she wore, and sometimes even the subject of her conversation as they imagine it to have been. She makes it her business to be seen everywhere, and she spares herself no fatigue. If she gives an "At Home," eager paragraph-mongers, insidiously invited for the purpose, deluge the editors with elaborate accounts of the party, the decorations, the dresses, and the refreshments. Her public importance is, in fact, the manufacture of the Society Press. But why it should be so is one of those problems which I must leave for discussion till I write my treatise on the "Anatomy of Society."

Then, I believe, I shall be able to satisfactorily prove that nobody is anybody, in a relative sense; but in the meanwhile, of course, everybody is somebody, in a journalistic sense.

For instance, the other night I went to Mrs. Vere Veneer's party at her large and sumptuously appointed house in Cromwell Road, and to-day I read in a descriptive paragraph that "everybody who is anybody was there." It is a triumphant phrase from the hostess' point of view; it is a seductive phrase to those whose ambition is social importance, for evidently to be seen at one of Mrs. Vere Veneer's crushes is to be stamped with personal distinction. Well, certainly till I read this paragraph I had no idea I was "anybody," nor, to tell the truth, had I any idea that Mrs. Vere Veneer herself—by the way, she was plain Mrs. Veneer in the old days—was anybody in particular. But there is a magic power of transformation in the pens of your Society journalists; they confer their own patent of notoriety.

But let me recall the motley assembly of the other night. There was a musical countess of Bohemian predilections, who was a centre of attraction to a number of professional musicians of more or less com-

petence—often less—and an exuberance of manner.
There was a funny little actor, who, finding himself for
a few minutes
unnoticed,
skilfully re-
vived attention
by some im-
promptu buf-
foonery with
a bust of a
negro in the
corner.   Then   a
languid vocalist, who during the evening rapturously whis-
pered his own mystical melodies, was sitting
in a corner absorbed in the conversation of an enthusiastic young girl, while many mothers of families,
some of them ladies of title, seemed to be jealously
watching an opportunity to lure the fascinating singer
to themselves.   And when one or two of them succeeded, how comic were their fawning attitudes of
triumph.

Then there were some lady-novelists, attended at a
respectful distance by their weary husbands, all alert

to talk about their works ; other writers who found everybody else overrated, and professed to despise popularity, or to regard it as a deadly microbe ; critics who grumbled at being expected to criticise things they were unaccustomed to, and others who protested that life was too short for anything to be endured which they didn't like ; and ladies who, while industriously making notes of the costumes of the guests, talked largely of the claims of literature and the power of the Press. There were one or two A.R.A.'s run to seed, and two or three members of the Emancipated Art League, who held that it was a higher testimony to true artistic merit to be laughed at by the *Times* than praised by Ruskin. There was a bountiful supply of " entertainers," amateur and professional, all ready to sing, recite, ventriloquise, or perform card-tricks on the slightest provocation.

There were a few civic dignitaries, doctors, lawyers, and divines with a penchant for the stage; some " Society Actresses " to give the affair style ; an Irish member or two, more or less connected with newspapers, the usual sprinkling of men about-town, who go "everywhere," and women of fashion, as reflected by the ladies' journals, together with an indistinguishable crowd of persons whose evening's enjoyment appeared to consist of asking, "Who is that?" and flattering themselves that they were in the company of genius and greatness. And this was "everybody who is anybody," while Mrs. Vere Veneer was the Madame Recamier of this latter-day *salon* of small "somebodies."

To many of her acquaintances who delight to be her guests, Mrs. Veneer is merely a social mushroom. They did not observe her social growth till she was a full-fledged hostess, giving "At Homes," to which they were ready to accept invitations. They know nothing of the patient struggle from obscurity; they saw not the persistent progress, step by step, towards the attainment of her ambition. To "get into Society" is, among the middle classes, the ruling passion in the average female breast, just as money-making is in the male. By getting into "Society" I do not mean necessarily being admitted into Court circles but the attainment of a more important social rating than the people next door, or being invested with a certain definite distinction that lifts one's name above the crowd.

Now Mrs. Veneer began by being nobody, socially

speaking. Her husband was a Midland manufacturer, in a fair way of business, and she had no knowledge of London Society and Bond Street dressmakers,
save through the medium of the ladies' journals,
which she devoured in discontent. But there came
a season of much profit to her husband's factory ; his
foreman of works had introduced a novelty which
became the fashion, and by aid of much advertising
the fortune of the Veneers was made. Then they
opened a branch house in the Metropolis, and Mrs.
Veneer insisted that their home should henceforth be
in London. Provincial life was ridiculous, she would
say, nobody knew anything in the country. She
yearned for society. She knew she was pretty, and
could wear a good gown with grace. She knew that
she had a bright intelligence, and that she was accomplished enough to be able to patronise the arts and
artists without betraying her provincialism. So her
husband, being well trained and not too assertive,
assented to the change of residence, and tried hard to
be content.

At first they had very few acquaintances, but among
them was one little woman, who was a host in herself.
She was an officer's widow, and though her means were

limited, her social connection was extensive. Her
gentility was unimpeachable, and she had the *entrée*
into many good houses, for she was a genial little soul,
and everybody was sorry for her, though no one knew
exactly why. She always seemed to be working at
something in somebody else's interest, and was largely
and energetically engaged in promoting bazaars and
balls in aid of philanthropic institutions, so that the
sympathy she evoked on their behalf appeared somehow to cling to herself. Besides, a busy woman with
a mission, especially a philanthropic one, always
commands a certain amount of respect. Now this
little person added to her other energetic impulses a
persistent passion for introducing people to one another.
That anybody of any kind of personality should be
introduced to her set, or be in her set, except through
her medium, was a personal vexation, even a sorrow,
to her; therefore she made it her business to know
everybody, and always to be on the alert for intro-
ductions.

Of course she asked Mrs. Veneer to one of her
afternoon-teas, and made much of her, for she was
wealthy, pretty, and presentable, and at a glance Mrs
Cordial perceived that it was Mrs. Veneer's ambition

to become a social personage. So she took upon
herself the pleasant, and not altogether unprofitable,
task of showing Mrs. Veneer about, and introducing
her here, there and everywhere, a service which the
wealthy manufacturer's wife recognised in many sub-
stantially generous ways. Mrs. Cordial, at the same
time, was able to become a benefactress of singers and
instrumentalists of the benefit-concert order, for Mrs.
Veneer, having at present few engagements for which
she had not paid. was, at the instance of Mrs. Cordial,
a prolific purchaser of tickets for concerts and recitals,
in addition to charity bazaars and amateur theatrical
performances. As Mrs. Cordial always took care to
impress upon the *bénéficiaires* the extreme financial
importance of Mrs. Veneer's acquaintance, they
eagerly sought the honour of an introduction, which
flattered her as a would-be patron of the arts, and
generally secured them engagements to sing or play
at her little dinner-parties or afternoon-teas.

And these were the germs of her present "crushes,"
yet was her social progress not rapid enough to satisfy
her ambition. So Mrs. Cordial proposed that her
protégée should invite to dinner the chairman of a
company of which her husband was an influential

director and who was an impecunious lordling of high
degree, while she would send invitations to some of
the most distinguished of her own acquaintances, on
Mrs. Veneer's behalf, to meet his lordship. At the
same time she recommended, as being more stylish,
the addition of the prefix Vere to the patronymic
Veneer. And a very gorgeous dinner-party it was ;
for Gunter's had *carte blanche*. I do not know why I
was among the guests, except that Mrs. Vere Veneer
wanted to show Mrs. Cordial that she, too, had friends
of her own who knew something of London and its
people.

I took into dinner an antagonistic old lady, who
seemed to think that nobody who had not been in the
army or the diplomatic service had any social existence
whatever. I candidly confessed I had been in neither,
and apologised for the abominable impertinence of
existing in spite of it, and then she relaxed sufficiently
to ask me, "Who *are* these Vere Veneers?" As she
was their guest, like myself, the question surprised me,
but I replied that they were a lady and gentleman from
the Midlands, whereupon she informed me that she
knew nothing of them, but had come there to oblige
her friend, Mrs. Cordial. When the ladies had left

the table, a man drew his chair up to mine, and
essayed a commonplace remark or two, then asked
me, "Who *are* these Vere Veneers?" He also had
come to oblige Mrs. Cordial, and so had three-fourths
of the guests.

Yet—would you believe it?—from that dinner-party
dates Mrs. Vere Veneer's rise as a London hostess.
Of course everybody did not discover, as I did, that
it was a kind of "complimentary benefit" party, but
the dinner and the floral decorations were talked
about, and Mrs. Cordial used her influence to obtain
paragraphs in certain gossipy papers, to the effect that
Lord Thingamy dined with Mrs. Vere Veneer, and
that there were also present So-and-So and So-and-So,
the best known of the guests, while the amiable
hostess looked charming in something or other.

Since that time Mrs. Vere Veneer has been able to
walk alone, and now she turns the tables, and "takes
up" Mrs. Cordial or not, as she finds it expedient. It
is now more useful to take a lady of title about with
her as a companion; and as she buys tickets for
everything, drives in handsome carriages, and always
collects about her a little coterie of pleasant people,
she never finds this difficult. It looks well in the

papers that "Mrs. Vere Veneer brought Lady Snooks,"
or that "those inseparables, Lady Clara Gushington
and Mrs. Vere Veneer, looked in on their way from
Mr. Lemon Yellow's Studio Tea." Mrs. Veneer
has acquired the habit of regarding everything from
the point of view of social advancement. She is of
the world worldly, and though her provincial simplicity has quite worn off, she maintains a universal
amiability that sometimes passes for it. She is
charming to everybody, and her hospitality is pro-
verbial, for she distributes her cards wherever she
goes, but not to any one whose name is never heard.
If she goes anywhere and there is an actor, an artist,
a musician, or even a journalist in the room, with
whom she was not previously acquainted, be sure you
will meet him at her next party. Of course, any one
who "receives" is promptly angled for, and they will
be mutually visiting each other before the week is out.
Mrs. Vere Veneer literally stalks drawing-rooms for
social entities or Bohemian "somebodies," and she is
so pleasant about it that nobody attempts to resist her,
and every one goes to her, and the lady-journalists look
upon her with a sort of reverence, and thank Providence
that there is a Mrs. Vere Veneer, for she is always

profitable "copy" to them. And, indeed, there be
many others who find her profitable, for she spends
much money in her endeavours to exploit Society. It
is an expensive business and a fatiguing, for she must
be always on the move, always on the alert for the
latest sensation. If a new form of entertainment for
evening parties arise, Mrs. Vere Veneer promptly
commissions one of the Bond Street agents to secure
it for her next "At Home." Failing this, she falls
back upon those of her professional acquaintances
who sing, or play, or ventriloquise for guineas and a
good supper.

They talk about Mrs. Veneer's parties, and there be
now those born in the purple who are pleased to find
them amusing, and it is said that next season Mrs.
Vere Veneer will be presented at Court by her friend
Lady Snooks—for a consideration. And who knows
but in a few years Mrs. Vere Veneer may be actually
received within Court circles, and play hostess to the
most illustrious?

And, in the meanwhile, what of Mr. Vere Veneer?
Is there a Mr. Vere Veneer? you doubtless ask, with
most people. Oh, yes; he is not much to look at, he
is rather *gauche* in his manner, and cannot wear even

D

Poole's clothes to look as though they were made for him, and his conversation is not very entertaining. But he pays the bills with prompt satisfaction, he tries hard to look as though he were leading the happiest life in the world, and he rejoices in his wife's successes, and cherishes every smile she spares him ; but when he can find an excuse to visit the mills in the Midlands, he does not hesitate to avail himself of it. However, as he does not know one from the other of the young men who follow in his wife's train, or of the women who are jealous of her gowns, or of the Bohemians who make themselves at home in his house, and as none of these ever seem to know him from Adam, he is satisfied to watch the comedy as a spectator, content so long as his wife plays her part well, and is duly applauded. If he appears on the programme at all it is simply as "the husband of Mrs. Vere Veneer."

THE DOMESTIC WOMAN

I ONCE heard a woman, whose only care in life was the effect she produced on her social surroundings, contemptuously describe Mrs. Hearthside as "a dull person who sits at home making flannel petticoats for the children, gives her husband his slippers, and has an egg with her afternoon tea." And, it is true, she does all this, and more. But I knew Mrs. Hearthside before domestic drudgery claimed her for its own; when she was a young romantic girl, to whom life presented a symphony of sweet possibilities.

She was the youngest of five daughters, and all had their admirers. To her the rivalry of the youths, who were proud to consider themselves her slaves, was a constant source of flattering amusement, but her heart remained untouched. If she saw any sign of real feeling on the part of any one of her swains, she was sorry, and her pity would perhaps incline her to

some show of tenderness, which was really but the
expression of her womanly sensibility, but it would
flatter the poor youth into fictitious hopes.   And then
the comradeship being disturbed by an intrusion of
sentimentality, she would discontentedly ask, "Why
cannot we be chums, without you pretending to be in
love and talking nonsense about marriage?"   And he
would sulkily answer that he loved her, and insist on
knowing if she cared for any one better.   When she
replied that she did not care for any one at all in that
way, he was not satisfied, but would sulk and reproach
her for not loving him, which irritated her.   Then she
would take to avoiding the love-sick youth altogether,
which would make him moody and disagreeable ; and,
her first pity having given place to disappointment, she
would seek to enjoy herself with newer "slaves," who
had not entered the sentimental stage.   But it was
always the same thing over again, they all went through
the various stages of comradeship, love, false hope, de-
spondency, and jealous moodiness, until she came to
the conclusion that the game was not worth the candle.
She was romantic, keenly susceptible to sentiment,
but her heart was still unmoved, sentimentality bored
her, passion was quite unknown to her, and she had

an ideal of love, born of day-dreams rather than of
actual experience. Her love episodes had hitherto
been pastimes, and the score had always counted
"one love."

But the days of her boy-lovers passed over, and, to
their despair, she ceased to take interest in any of
them, for a man's love had taken possession of her
soul, and opened the floodgates of feeling. The sweet,
latent passion of a pure woman's nature was awakened
by this love, and herself became revealed to her,
amazing her by the infinite range of feeling that
lay open. And yet life became narrowed to her,
for all the va-
rious interests
of her earlier
years were now
absorbed in the
one great passion
that made it appear
a divine blessing to
be alive. Nothing
seemed to matter
except that which concerned her lover, or herself in relation to him. Her love was her life;

and that fact comprised all that it was needful to know.

But he fell grievously ill and died, and she was left with only the sad memory of their love. She fully intended never to marry; but circumstances were too strong for her. The other girls did not "go off," and a family of five girls is a heavy responsibility for a father with a limited income. Something had to be done, and after all Dr. Hearthside was in a fair practice, and would certainly prove "an excellent husband."

Of course, ideas vary with regard to the essentials of an "excellent husband." With many persons the *desideratum* is reached when the tradesmen's bills are punctually paid, and there is no conjugal quarrel over the dressmaker's account. With some the model husband is he who belongs to no club, and always stays at home in the evenings; while others there are who consider that connubial perfection consists in the husband going his own way, and allowing his wife to go hers and find her own amusements quite irrespective of him. But there is really no fixed standard of excellence in husbands. The temperament, and even the temper, of the wife must determine this in each separate case.

Now, Dr. Hearthside was spoken of as an "excellent husband" in embryo, and many mothers angled for him, and their daughters encouraged hopes. He was a ladies' doctor, and his ways with women were soft and tender, his voice was musical and sympathetic, and his manner seemed to invite confidence and promise protection. Yet he was before everything professional. Tenderly as he seemed to treat them, women were to him interesting cases, psychologically as well as medically, and his lover-like methods were part and parcel of his practice. He knew women, and knew that personal confidence is half the battle in successful medical practice. Women always like to feel that a man is a possible lover, if even they only require his services as a doctor. They do not admit this to themselves, of course, but it is the case, for all that. Dr. Hearthside was deceptive; his tender manner with women covered merely a spirit of scientific investigation. When he was specially attentive to a woman—and his attention meant a sort of respectful devotion—he was deeply diagnosing her mental, moral, and physical condition; but she most probably thought he was making love to her. Mrs. Hearthside had been attracted to him in this manner. He found her melancholy, and she interested him as a study in disappointed love. He drew her out by speaking constantly to her about love, and she gave herself up gradually to his persuasive influence. She had hungered for love since death, by taking from her the man in whom her soul was wrapped up, had made life empty for her. She fed her heart on the memories of her love; but her soul had been awakened, and it yearned again for loving communion such as it had once known. Dr. Hearthside suggested the possibilities of love to her. When he analysed sentiment to her in quite a scientific way, her heart responded with emotion, for she thought he was pouring out his own eelings before her. So she consented to marry him, because she believed he could love, and love was the pressing need of her soul; while he, finding her a sympathetic and ready listener, and being pleased with her looks and her man ers, thought she would make an excellent doctor's wife, and help him to enlarge his practice through her social qualities. So these two married, and the love-dream of the girl died in the arms of the husband.

How many ideals are shattered by the intimacy of marriage, simply because the antenuptial love has been based upon fiction and misunderstanding. If only a man and woman made their several motives for marrying quite clear to one another, and were not so anxious to preserve a veneer of romance up to the very altar, matrimony would not be the terrible icono clast it too often is. Unless it supplies the true comple ment to a single life, of what value is it? It is all very well to talk about individualism, but every thing in the world is relative. The wife is what the husband makes her, and *vice versâ;* but the former is the more important consideration, since woman is more dependent. Pray forgive me, ye Amazons of the platform, ye of the Emancipated Sisterhood !

Mrs. Hearthside went to her husband with a soul yearning for poetry, and he gave her the plainest prose. The soft speech and gentle ways were for his patients, not for his wife. His domestic manner was as brusque as his professional was persuasive and engaging. He had no time to show his wife any of those little tender attentions which had previously touched her, and had made her recognise that this man might realise for her the dream of happiness which another had revealed to her. On the contrary, he did not take long to teach her that life was a scientific fact, specially intended to prove the value of the medical profession, and of Dr. Hearthside in particular; that all emotion was ridiculous, except in so far as it concerned a professional diagnosis, and that the aim and end of domestic happiness was to keep a comfortable home, and make a respectable show to invite patients. And for this she had given up the freedom of her soul; for this she had stopped all supplies of the love her nature needed. Henceforth her heart must feed upon itself, for Mrs. Hearthside holds very select views with regard to a wife's duties. If a husband do not answer all her spiritual longings, no other man must; if she cannot nestle her heart against his for warmth and comfort, her heart must go separate, cold, and lonely. Marriage has been a bitter disillusioning to her but she must bear with it, she must hide her romance away in the recesses of her memory, and live on the matter-of-fact of marriage, present a brave front, and pretend not to care, until in time, perhaps, she will delude herself into the belief that it is all the better so, at all events for her husband, and certainly for her children.

Happily, Mrs. Hearthside has several children, she has been a patient and considerate wife, and has contentedly accepted all the responsibilities of marriage. But when the children began to come Mrs. Hearthside's life really began to change. The interests of individual sentiment became absorbed in the preponderating interest of the nursery, and the woman was mother before everything; for children satisfied a craving which had grown out of the unanswered longings for a man's love.

So Mrs. Hearthside came to think of her children even before her husband; not that she ever neglects any one of his domestic comforts, or ceases to think of his professional interests—only his heart and hers have never mixed, whereas her children are part of herself. She feels that their lives are of her making, that their hearts are for her to feed with her own; that she is responsible for them, body and soul, and no nurse, no governess, could ever do for them all that she can. So she will spend her days with them in the nursery, see to every detail of their daily comfort, wash them, dress them, make clothes for them. If her husband wishes her to pay afternoon calls on patients whom he is particularly anxious to cultivate, she is sure to have to stop with Tommy, who shows signs of incipient whooping-cough ; or to take Cissie out to buy a new hat ; or to help Jack with his lessons. There is always something to be done for the children, or some housekeeping detail to be seen to which indirectly relates to them.

Dr. Hearthside is socially inclined ; he likes to go out and to receive friends at home. It is professionally beneficial, and it is amusing. He had hoped his wife would have been a useful aid in this matter, for when he married her she sang charmingly, and was quite an acquisition at social gatherings. But she had found that her husband took interest in her musical talent merely from the social *kudos* he derived from the possession of an accomplished wife. He only asked her to sing when they were in company, never when they were alone—then he had always work to do, which music would only interrupt. So she has ceased to cultivate her singing ; her voice became weaker after the birth of her babies, and now she only cares that it is strong enough to sing lullabies. And with the lessening interest in the artistic pleasures and emotional joys which had filled her girlhood comes an increase of interest in all the petty and prosy details

of domestic life. She has gradually grown to think of
nothing but her children, her husband's creature comforts, and her house. With a numerous family—for
the getting and rearing of children, and the keeping
them healthy and clean, has become the ruling passion
of her life—economic considerations have become
necessary in the conduct of the household, and questions of housekeeping expenditure have now more
interest for her than the title of the last new song.
She knows the prices of butcher's-meat, of groceries,
of everything, and will talk about them ; she will converse on servants by the hour, and so particular is she
in regulating her household that she will visit the
kitchen continually, with the resu't that she is obliged
to change her servants much more frequently than her
acquaintances of less domestic habits. But she has
now become chronically domestic, and the effect is at
times very trying, especially to her husband. She instinctively passes her hand over the banisters as she
goes downstairs, to see that they are clean. She
insists on putting up the clean curtains in the drawing-
room herself, just at an hour, too, when the De
Brownes are likely to call ; and she always keeps a
duster in the chiffonier for special use at socially in-

opportune moments. But, worst of all, she has become dowdy in her dress, and only cares that the children shall look nice.

Poor Dr. Hearthside, he never bargained for all this aggressive domesticity; but then, poor Mrs. Hearthside, she began married life with aspirations of a very different character. Her ideals are shattered, she has drifted into the purely domestic woman, simply b cause she married a man who misunderstood her, or rather who did not try to understand her at all after marriage. Women are very malleable creatures; Mrs. Hearthside might have been an ideal wife with another husband. As it is, to the many who see her only as she is now, she is simply an uninteresting specimen of a very common type—the domestic woman. Her soul is really only sleeping; let us hope that it will quite awaken again, when her daughters dawn into womanhood and her sons into manhood. Then her life will have new scope, and her own experience will stand them both in good stead. Will she strive that her daughters become not of this same type? Perhaps Mrs. Hearthside is happy in her way. Perhaps she considers her own state more enviable than that of a hopeless bachelor—like me, for instance. And perhaps it is; for in children we may live again. They are the resurrection of dead dreams, unfulfilled ambitions, and lost hopes. The domestic woman has this consolation, and so she has the better of us "who have free souls" —but no children.

A MODERN LADY-NOVELIST

IN the olden days, when fighting was the principal
business of men, and the womenfolk had nought to do
but stay at home and wait for the return of their lords,
all feminine imagination, stimulated by the songs of
minstrels, found vent in the weaving of storied tapes-
tries or silken scarves for the warriors. But in these
later days of peace and commerce and culture, when
wives are individuals, and not merely rated among their
husband's personal effects, and the measured roll of
the printing press is the voice of the civilised world, the
imaginative woman wields the pen, and leaves the
needle and the bodkin to her humbler-minded sisters.
So we have the lady-novelist, who is really the most
important and productive type of literary woman
But, when all is said and done, the ordinary lady-
novelist, who turns out her three volumes in accordance with the stereotyped taste of the novel-reading

clientèle of the circulating libraries, is scarcely much more interesting as a personality than the fashionable *modiste* who composes her costumes to suit the taste of her customers.

Mrs. Talespinner, however, is not of the ordinary type. She has a distinct personality of her own, and is altogether a remarkable woman. In every respect she stands apart from the brood of lady-novelists of the day; indeed, one might more aptly describe her as the lady-novelist of the day after to-morrow, so rapidly does she stride in advance of current feminine fiction. She belongs to the so-called realistic school and this has not yet been really invaded by women-writers, who are always more prone to conventionality than men, and as a rule, observe the sentimental association of facts rather than the facts themselves. Therefore, the appearance of a woman in the ranks of the "realists" attracted immediate attention, and the singularity of the position lent her works a *cachet* which their intrinsic force and cleverness confirmed. Mrs. Talespinner is a woman of quite conspicuous ability and extraordinary application, but she is a curious compound of weakness and strength.

Her mental vigour and intellectual strength are

E

remarkable, especially in a woman, but these elements
of power are qualified by the ease with which outside
influences, often weak in them-
selves, can switch her opinions
from one line of thought to
another. She will, on
this account, never be
a literary force, like
George Eliot, for in-
stance, or the Brontës. She has the audacity of
her opinions rather than the courage, for courage
implies strength, and in opinion she is weak; while
even her prejudices, of which she has accumulated
a plentiful store, are always wavering. But this
sensibility to influence is a useful quality in the
"realistic" novelist, though it may be damaging to
the literary artist. Now, Mrs. Talespinner is usually
true in observation and vivid in description, but this
frailty in the matter of opinion makes her uncertain in
the selection of her material. She is so afraid of
being conventional that she will treat subjects and
include details which perhaps delicacy not mere
prudery would suppress, which, however scientifically
interesting, may be contrary to the first principle of art,

namely, the producing of an impression of beauty. Yet Mrs. Talespinner is a woman of personal refinement, with a keen appreciation of the beauties of art and nature. As a novelist, however, her *métier* has so far been the startling of sensitive temperaments by wonderfully vivid descriptions of unpleasant characters amid unpleasant surroundings, without the omission of a single repulsive or disagreeable detail which could help to realise the story and its moral. For this reason there is a constant demand for Mrs Talespinner's books. The newspaper critics may abuse them, but the publishers keep a commercial eye upon them, and everybody reads them. Therefore Mrs. Talespinner may regard herself as a success.

So far I have told you about my friend in her literary, or, I may say, her public capacity only. But to really appreciate Mrs. Talespinner, one must know her in her home, one must have enjoyed her frequent companionship. Outsiders, who judge her only from the virile vigour of her writings, and the audacity of her subjects and their treatment, or those even who know her only through the daring frankness of her conversation, can have no idea of the essential womanliness of her nature. No woman, perhaps, ever so thoroughly got mentally on the outside of herself, and lived intellectua lly apart from her own womanhood. Thus she is a kind of female version of " Hyde and Jekyll," the Hyde being her literary personality, the Jekyll her sentimental self. It is, therefore, very difficult to know her as she actually is. She will, for instance, catch at some view of a subject which is in direct opposition to that held by those with whom she is conversing, and will obstinately argue it out, merely for the intellectual pleasure she derives from the independence of the position she has assumed. She may really be in exact accord with her hearers, but the delight to her of saying startling things, and of warring with words, is similar to that experienced by the skilful boxer in a bout with the gloves. But she is not a good stayer, and she is frequently beaten by an argumentative blow that is straight and strong, while she is honest enough to own her defeat afterwards, though perhaps not immediately.

She always relies on her strength. but yet knows her weakness ; for she will frankly avow that she is easily influenced. In the course of conversation, however, she will sometimes be carried away by fine-sounding phrases which, analysed, are mere verbiage. She will make statements which may be quite foreign to her real nature, and, to those who do not know her, she will convey an entirely false impression of her mental tone, though her mind will have flashed its vitality before them like a heliograph. The essential qualities of her mind, in fact, are catholicity of interest, active audacity, and the quickness and vividness with which she receives an idea, or perceives a fact, and passes it out again through the crucible of her own sentiency and experience. It is the same whether she be conversing on any topic of the day or writing one of her stories. The idyls and the epics of life, the romantic love-story, the heroism of noble souls, interest her without impelling her pen to activity ; but her literary and conversational enthusiasm is aroused by those sordid realities which the daily journals bring to light, by those stories of life in which the morality is crook-backed and twisted and the humanity limps with a cloven hoof.

Yet Mrs. Talespinner herself has none of these moral twistings, though it is through no fault of her own if opinions to the contrary get abroad ; for she has that perverse spirit which always prompts the excursionist to walk in those places where he reads that "trespassers will be prosecuted." True, this very spirit dates from Eve herself, but it is the key-note of the modern "realistic" novelist. Conventionality writes up the warning, and the literary realist defiantly trespasses, and takes the consequences, which are invariably notoriety and its attendant commercial success.

Mrs. Talespinne is, as a matter of fact, morally quite conventional, though she indulges in conversational and literary unconventionalities. But, fortunately, she has a husband who understands her as woman while he admires her as writer, being able to distinguish between her intellectual self and her sentimental. Thus he can sympathise with her literary ambitions without necessarily approving the results, and thus he finds happiness in his home, where a less discriminating and less generous man might find only domestic unrest. For with Mrs. Talespinner her literary work is the dominating interest of her life, though she will tell you, and convince herself, that all her ambition is centred in her little sons, whom she purposes educating with a view to their one day being Prime Minister and Lord Chancellor, as these, to quote her own words are " the only professions which

are not overcrowded." This is the extent of Mrs.
Talespinner's practical interest in her nursery—the
future careers of her baby sons. She does not spend
much time with them during the day, not that she is
not very fond of them, but children fidget her and
interrupt her writing. When, however, she does admit
them to her presence, she does not attempt to play
with them, but talks to them seriously and grandly of
her pride in their progress towards high estates, and
makes them promise, poor little mites! to be Prime
Ministers and Lord Chancellors, and instructs them
prematurely in their duties. As to seeing to the
details of their nursery existence—well, they have an
excellent and trustworthy nurse, and their father enjoys
that kind of thing. Hers is the pride and privilege to
care for them intellectually. She has made up her
mind that they shall be great men, that their greatness
may reflect upon her as their mother, and she candidly
tells you that she only wishes to write brilliantly and
successfully enough for people in after years to say,
"No wonder they are such talented men—they had a
clever mother."

Mrs. Talespinner's husband, by his perpetual patience,
good-humour, and large-mindedness, prevents his wife's

literary engrossment becoming domestically aggressive.
Like all women, when they undertake any professional
occupation, she is what one may call "shoppy." She
talks continually about her works in process of com-
position, and regards everything from the point of view
of "copy." Whenever she makes any new acquaintance who perhaps is not conversant with her literary
fame, she soon insidiously alludes to her writings, and
introduces quotations from them ; and then her husband, who is something of a wag in his way, will
seriously remark, "You may perhaps have gathered that
my wife writes a little," and then there will be a general
laugh, and Mrs. Talespinner's literary exuberance and
self-advertisement will pass as humorous, and become
a source of interest instead of boredom to her new
acquaintances. And one special virtue of Mrs.
Talespinner's is that she is quite as open to good-
humoured chaff as to criticism, and is as ready to
laugh at herself as at any one else. She has the *fin-
de siècle* lack of reverence, and will hold nothing sacred
from a joke or a humorous analysis—not even the
family dinner. Though she can order as good a dinner
as any one of my acquaintance, and has the worldly
wisdom to cultivate the constancy of an excellent cook

by allowing her to be the autocrat of the kitchen, she sometimes takes it into her head to direct the trades-men not to call for orders, as the ringing of bells disturbs her flow of thought. Then she quite forgets to send her directions until her husband comes home from the City and hungri y suggests dinner, which is consequently two or three hours late. But he, good-natured man, is quite satisfied to wait, so long as his wife has been content with her day's work.

Then her casual way of housekeeping occurs to them both as humorous, and perhaps while they are still at dinner the printer's proof of some serial story she is writing for a newspaper will arrive, and the rest of the meal will have to take care of itself. Surely her husband can help himself to the pudding; besides some day his amiability and devotion will furnish her with "copy," and how can she, when she comes to draw him as a character, describe his qualities with her customary graphic power unless she tests them under all circumstances? And her husband falling in with her literary humour, accepts all these things with equanimity. For he knows her, not only in her moods of literary enthusiasm or "shoppiness," or when she is playing with paradoxes and making sensa-

tional statements merely for bravado. He knows her
when she is wooed to gentler moods by the soft persuasive influence of the twilight, when the evening
star " washes the dusk with silver," and the realities of
life lose themselves in the mystic poetry of the hour,
and every feeling sings in tune the divine melody of
love, when the realistic lady-novelist, as well as the
woman of humble toil, mutely realises that it is a good
thing to be loved by a good husband and sweet children. He knows her then, and both are content for
always.

THE DISAPPOINTED SPINSTER

THOUGH I have always disputed the truth of the proverb that "the tailor makes the man"—since the more fashionably I am dressed the less I feel of my individual manhood—I am perfectly sure that the lover, not the dressmaker, makes the woman. As he pulls the strings of her heart, so can he shape her life, and according as he makes her love react upon herself with joy or sorrow, so can he develop the tendencies of her temperament, and, through all circumstances, bring out the sweet or the sour in her nature. Disappointment in love will embitter the cynical-minded woman as no mere loss of fortune could, and make her constantly aggressive in her attitude towards both her own and the opposite sex; whereas, to the woman of gentle faith, it will simply lend the crown of patient sisterhood with all men and all women, nor will it in the least destroy her faith in the beautiful beneficence

of the natural order of marriage. If you hear a spinster
who has passed her thirtieth year inveighing in set
and bitter terms against the joys and advantages of
the married state, be sure she has had her matrimonial
opportunity and missed it, while she gave the love of
her girlhood to a "detrimental."

> " Love will hover round the flowers when they first awaken ;
>   Love will fly the fallen leaf, and not be overtaken."

Miss Singleton is in the "fallen leaf" age, for the
sweet blossom-time of girlhood has long since passed
her by, and she has now seen some thirty-five summers.
Yet in many respects she is as young as ever, and
when she goes out to a dance she has no lack of
partners—and the best dancers too. mind you—while
on the tennis court she is always in much demand.
For she plays tennis with an activity and a style that
would put "sweet seventeen" to the blush, and the
rhythm and the vigour of her waltzing have outlived
the practical admiration of almost two decades of
partners. Indeed, not having the natural stress of
motherhood to bear, like those women who are wives,
Miss Singleton's physical energy and need of active
excitement still find vent in these pursuits, perhaps

with more zest even than in the days of her girlhood.

See her on the tennis court. She is completely
absorbed in the game, mentally and physically, and
any mistake on her own part, or bad stroke on the
part of her partner, provokes her to irritability. It is
something more than a mere game to her, it is the
supreme life-interest of the
moment. She must play
up with all her might
and main ; for life is
long and youth is fleet-
ing, and while she can
still run about, and
make swift, sure strokes
with her racquet, she can
make-believe to herself that she is not getting *passée ;*
but to give up dancing and tennis would be to confess
herself at once an old maid—horrible thought, and
quite absurd.

Why, look at her as she enters a ball room. Perhaps
there is just a suspicion of weariness and contemptuous
discontent in her countenance, but, the moment she
is recognised, a crowd of youths collect around her

clamouring for her card, and soon she is all aglow
with the excitement of the dance and the amusing
admiration of the dancing men.   They are only ingenuous youths, though, you will observe, or men who
regard women's society as a mere pastime.   They are
not the marrying men, not men who are seeking the
companionship and comfort of a wife.   Those are to
be found dancing with or talking to the young girls,
whose characters are not yet formed by time and
experience, who are therefore the more malleable
for the magnanimities of marriage, its responsibilities,
its sacrifices, and its necessity for mutual give and
take.   There is no sign of malleability about Miss
Singleton; there might have been once, ere the
gentleness of hopeful girlhood had been turned to the
hardness of disappointed womanhood.   But now men
do not think of her as a possible wife, or if they do it
is negatively.   "I like that Miss Singleton; she
dances splendidly, and can give you an answer back;
says devilish smart things too, but I pity any one who
married her: she would soon let him see who was
master, and it wouldn't be he."

Yes, Miss Singleton would require a very clever,
strong, and determined man to bring her into matri-

monial harmony now. She has acquired too much
of the habit of self-reliance and self-assertion ; a long
course of fruitless flirtation, in which she has fenced
both with experts and with amateurs, has caused her
to assume towards men always an attitude of defiant
defence, besides, the restlessness born of an unsatis-
fied life has become chronic with her. She is never
content to remain at home : her craving for amusement
and excitement is unceasing, and strangers rath r
than those who belong to her home-circle always
claim her first attention.

However charming and amusing she may be in
society, at home she keeps everything in a ferment,
and she is contented with nothing. She domineers
over her parents, as well as over her brothers and
sisters, her cousins, and intimate friends. She cap-
tiously criticises whatever they do, and wishes to rearrange and direct everything. She is jealous of her
relatives and friends who marry, though she constantly
avers that nothing would ever induce her to take unto
herself a husband, that the idea of a woman giving up
her personal independence and freedom to a man is
absolutely repulsive to her, while she professes a sort
of contemptuous pity for all those who do voluntarily

fall into this degrading condition. " Marriage is a snare for the weak-minded, and a delusion for fools," she will tell you, and she will pretend that she believes it.

But it was not always so. When I first knew Kate Singleton she was a bright, sympathetic girl of eighteen, and I envied the man who should some day call her his wife. She had certainly both will and character, but these were tempered by true womanly sensibility, and a good and magnanimous man's love might have helped her to develop into a delightful woman and an excellent wife. Unfortunately, however, the romantic element in her nature was appealed to by the fascinations of a man who was not good, though he understood women's weaknesses fatally well, and knew how to simulate the qualities that would most readily appeal to any particular girl. The cynical would perhaps excuse him with that cheap and common plea which covers so much of the wrong done in this world : " He was no worse than other men." He had certainly committed no crime ; only he had lived fast, perhaps a little faster than most men of his age. But he was a handsome young man, with a very engaging manner, a generous income, and many temptations ; so, of course, it did not take him long to spend his patrimony, though he enjoyed its full value in luxurious pastimes and dissipation. Then, having nothing but debts and a rake's reputation to his name, he endeavoured to make matrimonial capital out of his good looks and personal fascination. He met Kate Singleton, whose father he had understood would give her a handsome dowry, and perceiving the vulnerable place in her affections, he appealed to her sympathies through the story of his troubles and temptations. He worked with such infinite care and such insidious art, while he simulated the reckless, generous impulses of a simple-minded, honest-hearted hero of melodrama, that she gave her entire love to him, and became his promised wife Her parents opposed the marriage, seeing facts with the eyes of experience, but she held to her determination, defiantly proclaimed her faith in the man of her choice, and fought in defence of her love as fiercely as a lioness defends her cubs. Then all her womanhood was aroused, and mind and feeling put forth their strength for love had waked the heroine in her, and the spirit of romance exercised its magic influence upon her life.

But the **truth broke upon** her with sudden cruelty.

F

In an unguarded moment of anxiety concerning her
wedding portion, should she succeed in obtaining her
parents' consent, the lover revealed the mercenary mo-
tive of his wooing.   Her pride was wounded, her love
insulted, and by this lightning-shock all her better, truer
self was blighted in its growth.   All the taunts that
she had endured in defence of her love, all the sanc-
tity of feeling laid bare to the callous stare of this man,
recoiled upon her like the backwash of a wave of
bitter waters, turning all her sweetness sour.   Then she
grew to mistrust all men because of the falseness of
that one, and for a time she really set her face against
marriage, and that, too, when her face had yet the
bloom of girlhood upon it.

After a while, however, there came in her life an
Indian summer of love-longings and marriage-hopes,
but by that time the bitterness of doubt and disappointment had hardened the tone of her voice, drawn
her mouth to a set sternness, and tainted her mind
with cynicism.   So now, though there be plenty to
flirt with her, there be none who strive to lure back
the softness of her nature through the gentle persuasion of love, and no doubt she has recognised this,
for she always pretends to laugh at sentiment, and to

regard emotion as a species of hysteria. But once I chanced to notice her while a girl, with a voice that sounded like the very incarnation of music she was singing a simple, pathetic little folk-song.

It was out in a garden on a summer's night, "and music and moonlight and feeling were one," and, as Kate Singleton sat in the shadow of a tree, the tears rolled down her cheek, and I am sure that a sympathetic wooer might then have struck the vein of true womanliness in her with all the old softness, all the old lovableness of girlhood. But the melting mood was brief, for soon afterwards, in the gaslight of the drawing room, there were no traces of tears on her face, no gentle signs in her voice of a recent " session of sweet silent thought." She was busily challenging to flirtation a man whom she had artfully taken from the side of a pretty young girl to whom his words were as honey. It was a petty episode quite unworthy of her, for at best the conquest would be but for an evening, while it would cause the young girl a real heart-pang. But this was one of the atoms of excitement that make her life tolerable to her ; her dominant desire is to make men feel the pangs of unreturned love, or, failing that, her pleasure is to flirt with them

up to a point and then to turn round and snub them.
This affords her amusement as well as vent for
bitterness of feeling.

Some unmarried women can soothe their solitary
souls with charity of act and feeling, and bless other
people's lives with their benevolence, thus directing
the love and sympathy that one man has missed into
the wider channel of philanthropy. But these,
possibly, have never been crossed in love, or, if they
have, they are the women of whom the silent, uncom-
plaining martyrs of the world are made. Miss Singleton, however, is none of these. She cannot forgive,
especially as she finds it impossible to forget.

But after all, what is to be Miss Singleton's ultimate
aim in life? She cannot fill her whole existence with
dances, tennis, and flirtations, for time will have something serious to say on that subject. Say she is five-
and-thirty now; in another five years she will have
leisure from her present pastimes to realise her want
of new interests. She may not personally feel that
age is creeping on apace, but she will be made sensible
of the fact by all kinds of external signs. She will
find that, though the marriages of her brothers and
sisters, and other contemporaries of her girlhood, at

first made little difference in their attitude towards
her, the increasing and growing-up of their families
make a very great difference, and, naturally, the
interest that is taken in herself must under these conditions become gradually lessened. A new generation
of girls will have ousted her from the arena of flirtation,
for the spinster of forty stands but little chance against
the girl of twenty, though her wit be twenty times as
gr at, and her charms be all the more telling for long
practice. And then her interests will become narrower
as her field of interest is reduced in dimensions by the
encroachments of time and its consequences, until an
utter sense of loneliness and uncaredforness sets in,
and then God help her!

But I would let Miss Singleton's story point a moral
for all spinsters. Because one man gave her a bitter
draught to swallow, she allowed herself to believe,
until too late. that there was no more sweetness in the
world ; because one man proved false, she withdrew
her faith from all men ; and so she has missed the
blessings of domestic love, the wife's happiness, the
mother's joys, and so some good man has missed a
good wife.

THE INDIVIDUAL WOMAN

MISS STRONGITH'WILL believes in herself and has the courage of her individuality. She is no advertising advocate of Woman's Rights, as spelt with a capital W and a capital R; but she quietly asserts the right of woman to live her own life, to mould her own mind, to shape her own destiny, on equal terms with man, but in her own womanly way. She does not proclaim aloud from a platform that she has a mission; she makes no attempt at public philanthropy, and works among no paupers; she does not wear a divided skirt and ride far afield for notoriety; she does not lecture at learned societies; nor does she run about the world looking at loathsome diseases, and wheedling guileless journalists into writing her down a heroine. She is simply a woman who believes that woman's life can be quite complete without man, and she acts up to that belief by trying to make her own life self-contained and independent. To Miss Strongith'will the mere fact of being married or not is an extraneous circumstance, a matter of accident, opportunity, or inclination, which has nothing to do with a woman's individualism. She can assert her own entity, whether she has a husband or not. At least, this is Miss Strongith'will's theory, and she does not pretend to belong to the profession of strong-minded women. She has no sympathy with them; to her they are an impertinence, not because their minds happen to be strong, or perhaps unfeminine, but because they label themselves, and profess to despise any other brand.

Miss Strongith'will is the eldest of a large family; her parents are well provided with the means of life, their social position is such that the most refined and cultured society is open to them, and they have seen the wisdom and justice of giving their children the advantages of excellent education. In fact, the surroundings of Miss Strongith'will's life have been in every way conducive to the cultivation of her individuality. She has enjoyed the friendship of men and women of culture, and has had the advantage of contrasting them with the commonplace and the uncultured. She has had the invaluable opportunity

of travelling in foreign countries, not merely holiday
scampers through Continental towns, but sojourns for
months at a time in the very centres of the social,
artistic, and intellectual life of several countries, into
which she has been admitted on intimate terms.   She
has thus learnt to regard the world in a cosmopolitan
spirit, to look upon life in a large way.   She has been
forced to think for herself by the very eclecticism of
her training, but this very cosmopolitanism, while
enlarging her mind, has narrowed her heart to individuals.   It has made her difficult to please, and
impatient of any attempt to coerce her affections.   It
has deprived her of a husband.

Miss Strongith'will would be very indignant—very
angry if any one suggested that she ever wanted a
husband ; not that she has anything but respect and
admiration for the domestic affections, for the peaceful
beauties of home, for the lovely relations of parents
and children, brothers and sisters.   But she would
resent the implication that she could not have been
married had she so desired.   As a matter of fact, she
has had love affairs and offers of marriage ; but those
which she had before experience and critical judgment
had tempered her susceptibility, were of the ineligible

order—the medical student with a practice in prospect, the briefless barrister, the young artist who ought to be "on the line," if only the Academicians were not

so jealous, and so on. But these were in the days when a dance would lure her from any studies, when she was not above being flattered by the attentions of a "nice young man," and before she had realised that "life is earnest, life is real, life is not an empty dream." Now, however, she has become serious and superior, and the ordinary young man who flirts and dances and plays tennis is as nought to her. Men interest her, she says, intellectually, and only according to the measure of their mental powers or artistic sensibilities does she value their companionship. Let no man dare to talk frivolously to her; she would resent it as an insult to her understanding. If he attempted to pay conventional compliments, he would receive such a snub as should serve him for a lifetime, and put a check on the honeyed side of his tongue for evermore.

But Miss Strongith'will is not a stone, she is full of humanity, full of sympathy for those who suffer and those who struggle for existence or strive to realise lofty aspirations. She is only hard upon women who lower their natures for the love of men, who submit to martyrdom, or turn sour because they have been disappointed in love. She contends that love is not, as Byron has it, "woman's whole existence," but that, as the poet says with regard to man, it is of her life "a thing apart"—a beautiful thing that adorns her life and makes it more lovely, but not absolutely necessary as an active influence. But it could hardly be that a woman who thinks and theorises about love has never felt its magic spell, that she has never known the beautiful joy of loving and of being loved. Miss Strongith'-will's individualism is opposed to any outward show of emotion, and an ordinary acquaintance, even a friend, would never quite penetrate to her heart's secrets. She never talks of her love affair—her great love affair, I mean, which changed the girl to woman, and made her herself. But I know something of what it was to her, what she suffered with the disappointment.

He was not an ordinary lover, he was not an ordinary man. He was a visionary, a poet, a dreamer, with a genius for planning great works and achieving none. He was full of ideas, vague, beautiful ideas which remained abstract, but never took concrete form. He would conceive lovely lyrics, imagine glorious epics, dream splendid dramas—and write a few columns for the newspapers. He was always going to do something, but time went by, and he did nothing, that is, nothing worthy of his undoubted abilities. He started life with brilliant promise, and probably had he known Miss Strongith'will in the days of his promise, he might have given the world something to remember, but he was naturally indolent and terribly sensitive, he hated the actual labour of writing, and

the process of materialising his imagination, of re-
ducing his ideas to words, destroyed their charm for
him.   He would revel in a fancy, but he could never
satisfy himself in giving it form and expression, and
he would not expose to unsympathetic criticism his
dre ms and fancies in forms which did not fully
realise them.   Thus he was f ittering away his time,
his opportunities, and such talents as were his when
he met Miss Strongith'will.

He had just written enough in his time to reveal
latent possib lities of literary achievement, and his
poetic temperament appealed to her imagination.
It touched her sentimentally as she had never been
touched before, at the same time that it stirred her
intellectually.   She felt that here was a man with
talent, but without the requisite impulse of industry ;
what if she should make him achieve something noble
and endurable?   Like Keats, he declared himself for a
life of sensations 'a her than of thoughts.   She would
try and help him to combine both sensation and
thought, with the   result that he should produce
poems worthy to live.   His intellectual inertness
should be corrected by her strength of mind.   He
should yet be great through her sympathy, her aid,

her love. For she loved him; his very frailty of
temperament, his acute sensitiveness, his lack of self-
reliance, all appealed to her strong nature, and she
gave him that love which is all the deeper because it
feels bound to protect its object. But his imagination
was not satisfied by love of this order, it was not
sufficiently romantic, his temperament needed passionate response rather than intellectual aid. She
loved him entirely in her womanly way, and according
to the utmost possibilities of her nature, in which, however the intellectual element dominated the emotional,
whereas in her lover's nature it was the reverse. So,
while he grew impatient and weary, she began to
realise a sense of disappointment.

For a long time she hoped against hope that he
was really worthy of the love she gave him, that
he would do something to make the world respect
him; but he had encouraged his nature to yearn for an
ideal love, which should mean complete mutual self-
surrender, the making of two lives one. The idea of
female individualism he admitted was just, but it did
not suit him, the substitution of intellectual sympathy
and serene sentiment for that passionate love which
must absorb every function of soul and body, left his

life still unfulfilled. Literary achievement and fame could not fill it, only woman's love could do that, only the love that maintains no distinct individuality, the love that gives and takes all. Aspasia would have suited him, as Walter Savage Landor draws her. "We cannot love without imitating," she says, "and we are as proud in the loss of our originality as of our freedom." But this was not Miss Strongith'will's way of loving; to lose any measure of one's individuality even in love was, in her eyes, to be degraded. Yet she loved deeply in her way, and when her impressionable, idealist lover, without any thought of inconstancy, took his love to another, whose nature he deemed more in sympathy with his own, Miss Strongith'will suffered a bitter blow and a deep wound.

She uttered no complaint, however, and few ever knew that she had been in love, much less that she had found it disappointing. But the experience seemed to open out her life, she saw clearer, her knowledge of human motives and feelings was widened, and she felt more than ever that woman can live individually and independently. She did not, however, perceive that she had met her disappointment

through not attempting to weld her own individuality
with that of the man she had loved without understanding. But after that she believed implicitly in
herself, and determined to follow her own pursuits, to
live as independently as if she were a man, and,
thrown on her own resources, compelled to earn her
own living, a duty she considers every woman owes to
herself.

What would be Miss Strongith'will's views on individualism were she a happy wife and the mother of a
large family, whether she would still consider that a
woman has the right to live exclusively according to
her own tastes and inclinations, I cannot tell; I think
she would find it rather difficult in practice. As it is,
however, Miss Strongith'will is happily situated, for
she is the beloved of her immediate family, among
whom she is regarded as a superior being who ought
to have her own way in everything.

She is the oracle of the house, and she rules accordingly. Perhaps her constant habit of self-reliance has
made her a little dogmatic and impatient of contradiction. She has the courage of her own opinions,
and the pugnacity of them. It is not wise to differ
from them unless you be prepared to pummel her

with logic and authority. Then you may have a
chance with her in argument, but with all her strength
of will and self reliance, she is a very woman, and her
reason will often be none but a woman's reason, " I
think it so, because I think it so." She "sees life
steadily," and if she does not see it quite whole, she
certainly has a good view of it, and from her coign of
vantage she perceives the devious ways of women who
have no vocation. Therefore, she devotes herself to
art as a profession, with just the same enthusiasm as
a man of fortune strives in the City to increase
his banking account. She has not the stimulus of
necessity, but she feels a certain triumphant satisfaction in doing what she is not obliged to do.

She has artistic aspirations, why should she not
pursue them with as much avidity as if her livelihood
depended upon her success? Why, she argues, should
a woman only take to professional work when she
cannot depend upon men to work for her? And why
should she be accused of taking the bread out of
poorer women's mouths because she sells pictures,
when her father or husband is able and willing to give
her as much as she wants? No, Miss Strongith'will
realises the sordid fact that money is the chief incen-

tive to all work, and that work is valued according to its price; therefore she claims the right for women to work for money according to their instincts, abilities, and inclinations, without exciting any more remark than a man would who worked under similar circumstances. But though Miss Strongith'will asserts woman's right to independence and the courage of her individuality, she is none the less womanly, none the less gentle and steadfastly affectionate to those she knows intimately, and those who understand her. Would she have been more so had she been happily married, so that her own individuality had blended harmoniously with that of the man she loved,- and had become greater for motherhood? That is the question.

THE SUBMISSIVE WOMAN

I REMEMBER, when I was a little boy, a beautiful young woman and a very handsome man coming to my father's house, and these were husband and wife. And I looked upon him with a sort of worshipful wonder, for they told me he was a brave soldier, and had fought gloriously in battles. At that period of my life my young imagination was quickened by every story of adventure, and the only books or pictures that appealed to me were those that told of battle, or of the doughty deeds of soldiers and sailors. The sword seemed to me then far mightier than the pen, which latter I regarded merely as an instrument of scholastic torture.

Imagine my great pride and joy, therefore, when this real live hero talked to me as familiarly as any schoolboy of my own age, and when, looking over some pictures of the Crimean War and Indian Mutiny, which were among my treasures, he told me how he had stormed the heights of Alma and captured Sebastopol, how he had relieved Lucknow, and blown thousands of mutinous Sepoys from the guns. I listened to him with all my sense and spirit. How graphically he described the fights, remembering every detail, even to the name of the little bugler who sounded the "cease firing," and the exact expression of the Sepoys the moment before the guns were fired that should blow them to eternity! I drank it all in, and thought there never was such a great man in the world as Captain Marshall Meek. No wonder that his sweet and gentle wife cast such constant looks of affectionate pride upon him. She was indeed a fortunate woman to be the wife of such a hero, and I regarded her with boyish enthusiasm, because of her heroic husband's reflected light. To me they were the most romantic couple I had ever met, for they embodied beauty and chivalry — such as I had read and dreamt of. They might have been Lancelot and Guinevere for me and they remained impressed upon my young memory, she as the beautiful daughter of a distinguished family, he as an ideal soldier, handsome and brave.

I did not see them again till I had reached man's

estate, and then they came once more to my father's house.   But what a change had the years wrought! He was now a shaky, middle-aged man, with alternate intervals of boisterous merriment and ill-temper, and only the reminiscent suggestion of his old gallant bearing and good looks; while she was an absolute wreck of her former self.   Her fair, plump features were now sallow and shrunk, her bright, gentle countenance told of nothing but sorrow, suffering, and anxiety; her full, elegant figure had become attenuated beyond recognition.   The old regard of proud affection had given place to a haunted, restless look of fear, of expectancy of something terrible.   Yes, a few years had transformed the gallant soldier into a confirmed drunkard and bully, and the poor wife into his abject slave.

It was a pitiful story.   He had had a sunstroke in India—the original excuse of so many drunkards — and a craving for stimulant had succeeded.   Stronger and stronger grew the craving, weaker and weaker the power of resistance, until the habit of drink became so strong that the case was quite a scandal.   " Con duct unbecoming an officer and a gentleman," was the official designation given to the offence for which he

was cashiered from the army, and social ruin was
the result. And down with the disgraced man went
the wife and children. Society always
generalises, and the stain of a name
clings to the innocent bearers of
it. Of course people pitied poor
Mrs. Meek, but with such a
husband who could visit her?
So, with ruined career, with
name disgraced, with shattered constitution, Captain
Marshall Meek brought his family home
to England, and by undue extravagance and gambling
speedily exhausted the income his wife had brought
him as dowry. His social disgrace seemed to have
made him desperate - his weakness for drink certainly
rendered him insensible to all the finer feelings of
manhood, and he spared his wife no humiliation.

She was the daughter of a proud and distinguished
man, who had won his baronetcy by splendid services
to the State, whose father and grandfather before
him had won honourable reward from a grateful
country. The men and women of her family were
proud and spirited to an unusual degree, and when

she went to them, socially and financially beggared, to ask assistance for her children, they answered her that she must separate herself from her drunken and disgraceful husband, and then they would see what could be done for her.

But Mrs. Meek was wife before everything ; whatever her husband had done, however he might drag her and their children down, whatever he might make her suffer in body and spirit, she was still his wife, and as she had vowed at the altar to love, honour, and obey, so would she strive to fulfil her vows. Therefore pitying and forgiving those of her kinsfolk who had urged her to what she considered the breaking of the marriage vow, she gave up all hope of their assistance, and determined to try and eke out what little was left of her fortune as best she could. Her pride had been sadly humbled, but she still had a remnant of independence. She still hoped to redeem her husband's reputation, and woo him from the injurious ways of drink.

It was at this period that I met again the hero and heroine who had so captivated my boyish fancy, and never shall I forget the shock of recognition. They seemed to have been transformed by some sort of metempsychosis-while-you-wait process. The Captain's old buoyancy had given place to irritability pretending to be joviality—a miserable sham, practised exclusively for company. And this seemed to alarm his wife far more than his outbursts of drunken passion, for then she knew that the bully was uppermost, while the cunning of his pretended humour puzzled her, and kept her upon tenter-hooks, fearing what he might say or do.

It was a miserable life for her, poor thing. She, who had lived her youth in luxury, and her early married life in comfort and amid brilliant social surroundings, was now compelled to endure every degradation that genteel poverty and social vagabondage could inflict. They were very poor, yet her good-for-nothing husband insisted upon an outward show of gentility which he had not the grace to support. He would drink in private and in public, he would debase his manhood, and bully his long-suffering wife, but he would drain the very scanty family purse to preserve a pretence of social position. The children were growing up, but little were they heeded, except as servants and errand-boys. Education befitting the sons and daughters of an "officer and gentleman" was out of the question; all the cash that could be squeezed out of the domestic exchequer was appropriated by the Captain for his personal expenses, his clothes, and his drink. Poor Mrs. Meek had to find clothing for the boys and girls as best she might, just as she had to keep the household going. For herself, one or two black silk dresses which had seen better days served her through years of humiliation. She had lost the semblance of gentility, and only tried to make herself look a little smarter when her husband rated her for forgetting her position. Her position, indeed!

And she submitted to all this humiliation, she allowed herself and her children to be dragged down lower and lower, she offended beyond reconciliation the rich, proud relatives who could have helped her, because they expressed their just resentment against her husband and their indignation at her obstinate martyrdom, all simply for love of this man who was quite unworthy of it. She had never heard of Individualism; the thought of a woman having a free soul, with an independent life of her own to work out, had probably never entered her head. She was one of those women who think that the whole duty of woman is towards her husband, be he good or bad, tender or cruel, devoted or selfish. That he has broken his marriage vows does not relieve her of the obligation of hers—she must be faithful to the end. And so Mrs. Meek suppressed her independent womanhood for the sake of a worthless man. There was no question of clinging to an ideal of her girlhood, that was broken long since, and Mrs. Meek was not an idealising woman; she saw things as they were, but she thought it was her duty to try and soften their brutality. If there was little of the old love remaining, there was the old slavish devotion, and the submission of her individuality to his caprice. She retained the mediæval notion that the husband was the wife's lord and master, and when misfortunes, albeit of his own making, came upon him and involved her, she considered that it was all the more obligatory for her to unself herself, so as to give him the more consideration. She had joined her lot to his for better or for worse, and, as she would not have thought of leaving him had it been better, she would not desert him when fortune was at its worst. Let him humiliate her as he would, she would be a martyr in the sacred cause of wifely devotion.

There are some women who must be martyrs at
all cost, if not in earnest, then in make-believe.
Generally there is more folly and egotism in their
martyrdom than high-minded purpose, but sometimes
there is a touch of the genuine angel. Now, I never
met a more serious martyr than Mrs. Marshall Meek,
and if there was a good deal of the fool about her self-
sacrifice, there was something, too, of the angel-- no
ordinary woman could have been so absolutely without resentment with so much just cause. Whatever
she suffered, and Heaven knows she must have
suffered as few women in her station of life are called
upon to suffer, never was she known to utter complaint. No indignity, no deprivation, could provoke
her to reproach her husband ; and when I have heard
her sons and daughters grumble at their position, she
would always chide them gently, and expect pity for
their father's misfortunes. For herself she sought none.
God in His own good time would pity her, she would
say, till then it was her duty to submit patiently.

But was this just either to herself or her children ?
For herself, it must rest with her own conscience
whether she has made the best use of her life, debas-
ing her soul to the service of a worthless man, be he

husband a thousand times over. But for her children, has she not grossly abused her responsibilities? She has sacrificed them to a father who has squandered the most brilliant opportunities, and degraded all their lives. Had she agreed to the wishes of her relatives to separate judicially from her worthless husband, whose downward course she was powerless to stay, she might have restored her children to their proper social position, and secured to them all the advantages of education. But she allowed herself to become estranged from those who could have helped her, and to beg for alms from friends whose purses were of less capacity than their hearts. And, oh! the terrible struggles of her life, the humiliation, the injustice, the pity of it.

Then when the inevitable *delirium tremens* cut off, in what should have been its prime, a life once so full of promise so grievously unfulfilled, it was all too late to repair the terrible mischief done. The children, who had been dragged up anyhow, lived anyhow, and were married anyhow to those who dragged them down still lower in the social scale. And their mother, the widowed martyr to her sense of wifely duty, ignored by proud and offended relatives, neglected by children whose gratitude she had never encouraged, and, weary of all, has hidden herself away in some obscure lodging to await, as patiently and submissively as she has lived, the coming of easeful death.

And there will always be women like this to soften men's lives by their own self-submission ; but, thank goodness, there be also women who know how to live their own lives, and to stimulate, as well as smooth, the lives of men.

THE "AWFULLY JOLLY" GIRL

MABEL FLIRTINGTON is still in the age of gigglehood, a period of life through which every well-regulated girl must pass. If a girl cannot enjoy a good giggle, there must be something very much the matter, she must be suffering severe personal affliction of some kind or another, or, may be, she is a changeling, or perchance the stars went wrong at her birth. A positively serious young girl is an anomaly; she cannot be tolerated. Youth is naturally joyous, and, if the girl be mother to the woman, what a depressing maturity will be that of the girl who cannot giggle. I say this because I have frequently heard *passée* women and disagreeable men speak contemptuously of the "giggling girl," and with great injustice. I reverence youth myself, and in this I imply no disrespect to old age, which, when it is delightful, is delightful indeed, though old people are not always companionable.

Young people, on the contrary, have not had time to lose their illusions or to suffer all the ills that age is heir to. Nor, on the other hand, have they acquired the wisdom, charity, and experience of years; therefore they offer the charms of simplicity, frankness, and enthusiasm. Their companionship is a refreshment, and I am prepared to endorse all that the poets have written in eulogy of youth.

I have a firm faith in the poets; they anticipate all my noblest thoughts, and all my freshly perceived truths. So when Tom Moore long ago sang "There's no hing half so sweet in life as love's young dream," he merely expressed my present opinion. But one only fully realises the inestimable beauty and value of youth when one's hair is getting thin on the top, one's ruddy-brown beard is beginning to melt into grey, and one's limbs do not move as actively as of yore. It is middle-age, not old-age, that really laments over lost youth. Old age has almost forgotten its charm, and only wants peace, quiet, and comfort; but middle age is still active enough to want to be younger. It is a beautiful thing to be young, and have all our responsibilities in embryo, with all the world before us, fair and full of hope, promise, and possibility. I think there is no more engaging sight than a pretty girl at her first ball, or a gallant youth in uniform for the first time. They are ready to conquer the world, and perhaps after all they only make a conquest of each other, but they are just as happy.

When I get into one of those melancholy moods to which lonely bachelors are occasionally liable, nothing so effectually restores me to my usual equanimity as a verbal rally with Mabel Flirtington. She is of that essentially British type of young lady that may be classified as the "awfully jolly" girl. I do not believe you would find a Mabel Flirtington of any other country in the world. She is indigenous to the British Isles, and the British Isles can boast no richer product than the "awfully jolly" girl.

Mabel Flirtington is an *ingénue* of the most *fin-de-siècle* order, one with a will of her own and a brain that is wide awake. Indeed, she is a natural product of the time that makes for individualism in both sexes. She is bored or amused with equal discrimination, and selects her own entertainment and occupation accordingly, just as she selects her own friends. She has a keen sense of humour and a power of sarcasm, and, as she is always on the alert for any fun, and ever ready to dare anything requiring pluck and strength, she is the admired of all youthful admirers. There is not an honest-hearted, clean-minded young man of Mabel's acqu·intance, or a girl that is worthy of a man's respect, who will not without hesitation describe her as an "awfully jolly" girl, by which is meant all that is frank, and brave, and comradelike. She is a girl to command instant respect and admiration from all those capable of understanding her; but to the meaner-minded she will present no favourable view, for she will tread on their mental corns, so to speak. Her self-reliance will to them appear mere conceit, her ready repartee will sound like impertinence, and her fearlessness seem only swagger.

For myself, I love to see Mabel among a number of young folk, to hear her asserting the profound opinions of eighteen, and to watch how her very attitude of independence lends persuasion to her illogi-

cal utterances. I enjoy her ingenuous way of playing
the despot, and it is delightful to see how thoroughly
she recognises her power, and how she revels in its
exercise. Last year was her initial "season," and yet,
to see her at her first ball, to witness the experienced
skill with which she played off her partners against
each other, amusing herself by lighting little sparks of
jealousy, and then discreetly fanning them into tiny
flames sufficient to leave burning embers for the next
occasion, one might have imagined she had been going
to balls for years past, and had served a long apprenticeship in flirtation. Mabel adores dancing with all
the enthusiasm of eighteen, but she is nothing if not
candid, and she told one partner bluntly that she
would rather sit down as he could not dance, and
then she signalled to me, as an old friend, to go and
rescue her. Mabel was certainly the most self-
possessed *débutante* I ever saw—the end-of-the-century
ingénue is never shy, mark you- and she made more
harmless heart-havoc in a single evening than her good
Aunt Gertrude had made in a lifetime.

The position of father confessor to an erratic
young lady like Mabel is not a very difficult one, for
her confessions are very innocent, although she some-

times thinks she is making terrible avowals, but they
are at least exceedingly amusing. She flirts for pure
fun and sport, there is no question of heart in it.   Her
heart she keeps for something more serious, though
she does not know that– she is not yet awake to it,
and I doubt if she thinks at all seriously of the possibilities of love and marriage. Certainly at the present
time she has no desire to be married, although I know
one or two goodly youths who entertain hopes of her.
Not that she gives them any encouragement; on
the contrary, she delights to tantalise them, and
which of them, if any, will be the successful rival I
scarcely think she quite knows herself, though one
may guess.   However, at present she only regards the
tender passion from the point of view of entertainment, and as accessory to the more serious pursuits
of riding, boating, tennis or dancing. These are the
business of her life, and she will tire herself utterly in
pursuing them.   Flirting is merely a relaxation.

   To see Mabel at her best, you must be with her
up the river. You must see the dexterous manner
in which she handles her canoe, or the graceful
skill with which she propels her punt. An artist
who should make his happy sketching-ground that

particular part of the Thames where Mabel spends the
summer months, and should persuade her to submit
to being frequently sketched, might bring away a veritable wealth of pictorial material. He would have to
be up very early in the morning to see her, in her
dainty red bathing costume, take her matutinal dive
from the landing stage opposite the cottage where she
stays—though he had better not let her know he is
within sight, for her swimming is the admiration of
only very privileged connoisseurs.

Then he should see her paddling her canoe up
stream, her red shirt and the crimson cushions making
a brilliant note of colour against the dark green of the
foliage on the banks. If he watch till she turns round
the bend near the lock, he will see some canoeing of
no amateurish kind, for those rapids make heavy
demands on the pluck and skill of the fair canoeist.
That is the place to sketch her, for it is a ready-made
picture. Then let him see her, later in the morning,
mounting her horse for a canter across country, with
so sure a seat and such a command of the animal, one
would not be surprised to see her flying over any five-
barred gate. What a look of pride is on the face of
the young cavalry officer who rides by her side; for

not another fellow in the regiment ever rode out with a finer horsewoman, or a prettier girl to boot.

Then, again, what a picture she makes, as, flushed with her ride, she leaps from her saddle, and holding her habit with one hand, she strides up the garden walk, with her dogs bounding by her side and jumping for her caresses, for she loves animals as they love her. Could any painter wish for a more perfect type of pure, healthy girlhood ? Perhaps, though, he will see more opportunities for his pencil when, clad in a loose fitting silk shirt of old rose colour, and a white alpaca skirt, she is displaying all the supple grace of her figure on the tennis lawn. How active she is, how skilful and confident her play, how her face glows with pleasure and excitement, and with what cheery banter she keeps up the spirit of the game. While she is playing her personality dominates the lawn, for every bit of her vitality goes into what she is doing at the moment ; while she works physically at the play, her merry little mind is finding vent in a quip to this player, a bit of playful sarcasm to another, or a repartee to some comment from the onlookers. No wonder that after tennis she may be seen lolling in a hammock, under shady trees, fast asleep. And how lovely she

looks! Our friend the artist should come upon her
there, and make a study for a Sleeping Beauty, for
painter's fancy has never yet done justice to the
subject, and never will, until he paints the beautiful
princess as a fair English girl, asleep in a hammock
in a shady garden by the silver Thames.

But he must make haste with his sketch, for the sun
is going down, and, as the sweet, grey evening comes
on apace, Mabel awakes refreshed from her half-hour's
nap, makes her way down to the water, and springs
into her punt. The young soldier lounges on the
cushions, and she, pricking the bed of the river with
the long bamboo, sends the flat-bottomed craft through
the water with splendid speed, while her grace and
strength suggest some Greek athlete of old rather than
a modern English girl. Her figure, with the long pole
in her hands, stands out clear against the sky, which
is brightest in that hour " between the moondawn and
the sundown," when the spirit of romance is beginning
to flit about, whispering its secrets to those hearts that
are will ng to hear. And who knows whether Mabel's
heart hears or not? She is dreamily silent, and the
idle youth in the punt has been bluntly told not to talk,
for he could not interpret for her the beautiful mysteries

of this hour, "when the twilight hangs half starless"
She is not sentimental, and the romance of her life is
as yet the romance of comedy ; but there are moments,
even for an "awfully jolly girl" like Mabel, when the
simple eloquence of Nature is all-sufficient, and any
ordinary talk is an intrusion.

Now Mabel takes her punt up a picturesque bit of
backwater, where the trees stretch their branches
across from bank to bank and clasp each other, and
the water-rats are boldly sportive, and here she stops
nd listens to the many-voiced silence, forgetful of her
companion. But the spell of the hour and the river is
upon him, and in his boyish blundering way he blurts
out his love and asks Mabel to marry him—which is
just the last thing he should have done under the
circumstances, if he wanted to remain "chums" with
her. As it is, he puts her out of humour, and she
makes for home as speedily as possible. Then these
two do not speak all the evening ; she devotes herself
to somebody else, and he is very wretched. Next day
she does not ride with him, nor does she take him out
in her punt. At last he has to beg her forgiveness,
which she grants on condition that he never talks
"nonsense" again. But they have not been quite on

the same frank terms since, and I hardly think they
ever will be again unless he remains constant for a
little while—say two or three years, perhaps—and
bides his time to ask her again.

There is a sweet and tender strain of womanliness
in Mabel's nature, and when, as her amateur father
confessor, I questioned her about her obvious difference with the young soldier, and she told me the facts,
I fancied I recognised a tone of pity not unmixed with
pleasure, which augured well for the boy's chances.
She is a wilful, erratic, delightful girl now ; and I feel
sure she will make a splendid woman. Cares and
sorrows will overtake her soon enough, and force upon
her the serious side of life, and her womanhood will
not fail to rise to the occasion. In the meanwhile,
let her continue to regard the world as a playground
where all is sweetness and light and pleasure. Let
her retain her illusions as long as possible, and enjoy
the delights of girlhood. Let her, in fact, extract all
possible pleasure from any sport, any amusement. It
will all react beneficially on her nature, and, when she
awakes to the responsibilities of life, she will bear
them all the more cheerfully that her youth has been
happy and uncrossed and "awfully jolly."

THE NUN

STRANGE as it may
sound, some of the happiest hours
I have ever known have been spent
within the precincts of a convent, while of the
friendships which have been a joy in my life, none
has made me prouder than that of Sister Annunciata.
It may appear curious for a man-of-the-world to count
a nun among his friends, but no one who has not
been privileged to enjoy it, can understand the pure
solace of conversing familiarly with a woman who,
having renounced the world for what she deems a

higher purpose of life, lives entirely apart from our
every-day existence, and has no intercourse with it
save through the ingenuous medium of young girls'
gossip. For Sister Annunciata belongs to one of
the educational orders of sisterhood, and, though she
has taken solemn vows for life, and may never go
beyond the boundaries of the convent grounds, or
again come in contact with the passions and ambitions inseparable from the struggle for life, she yet
has a fruitful field of affection among the convent
pupils, and thus she keeps her human sympathies
in constant activity. Moreover, Sister Annunciata is
the favourite of the convent, the beloved of all the
girls, and though this naturally leads to certain
jealousies, this very human trait of human nature
makes an effective contrast with the general placidity
of the place. The perfect faith in Divine grace, which
is the ruling spirit of the convent, appears beautifully
wonderful to one who moves amid the scepticism of the
age, but how much more beautiful is it in conjunction
with the humanity of these girls, their jealous love for
their favourite nun, her impossible efforts not to show
preference, and the striving of the other nuns to be
equally loved? Though they have given up the large

world, they have still their own little one. The beautiful natural craving for affection will not be renounced.

It was Sister Annunciata's supremacy in the regard of her pupils that procured me her friendship, for, being on a visit with some friends in the neighbourhood of the convent, the young daughters of the house were eager to take me to see their "dear Sister Annunciata." They were never tired of talking of her, and of the many virtues which endeared her to them, and they would not rest until I knew her too.

The idea of visiting a convent, and talking to a real live nun, was peculiarly fascinating to me, for my notions of convent life were vague and mysterious, and I regarded all nuns as uncanny creatures, living dismal lives in chilly cloisters. That they had renounced the world was sufficient, in my eyes, to invest them with a kind of unearthliness. Therefore, I approached the convent with a weird curiosity which I cannot describe.

The convent stands amid beautiful spacious grounds, composed of lovely gardens, groves, and grottoes, all picturesque and peaceful, with splendid views of sea

and mountain around. As we entered the gates, and
walked up the broad path leading to the grey stone
building, the calm influence of the place began to
work its spell upon me, and, as I saw here and there
among the trees the black figures of the nuns, walking
singly or in couples, suggestions of mediæval romance
flitted across my mind. It was vacation time, all
the pupils, save one or two, who were orphans, had
gone to their homes, and the nuns were enjoying
their hours of relaxation in the sunshine. There
seemed to be a quiet happiness about the place,
which quite upset my preconceived notions about
nunneries.

The parlour in which we awaited the coming of
Sister Annunciata, was severely simple in its furniture
and adornment. But as soon as the Sister entered, I
forgot the plainness of the room. I might have been
sitting on the most luxurious couch, instead of a stiff
horsehair chair, for all it mattered. She seemed to
exhale a sweet cheerfulness, and the room was filled
with a personality and a life that were entirely new to
me. She greeted my girl-companions with warm
affection, and joined in their girlish jokes, while she
talked to me with an absolute frankness and simplicity

I had never met before. She led us out into the grounds, and her merry laughter sounded strangely incongruous with her sombre garb, but as we walked along, I noticed that all the other nuns seemed anxious to show that they were quite happy. And, verily, they seemed so, as they walked among the flowers, or plucked the fruit, or read their books in shady spots, or basked in the sunshine, and talked or meditated. One of them, a good-natured, round-faced nun, who had been gossiping gaily with my young friends, but had for a long time kept shyly aloof from me, suddenly came up to me and told me that they were all as happy as the days were long.

And it was a place to be happy in, I thought, as I stood in a beautiful grove, where the sunlight peeped through the trees and patched the grass with silver, near to a little sloping eminence whereon rested the chapel, in which the dead Sisters sleep eternally, while beyond some yellow cornfields reached away to the grey walls that marked the convent boundaries, and the further hazy blue sea appeared to carry the picture away into dreamland.

And here, I reflected, these women live away from

the world we know, and they find happiness without
a struggle, without—but Sister Annunciata is standing
by me, and perhaps at this moment she is thinking of
the old days before she gave up her life to religion.
Yes, I have been talking to her of the outer world,
and have named one that she knew long ago as
a youth, and I tell her he is now a famous man.
And the mention of her boy-playmate awakens old
memories, and she tells me of her girlhood.

We are always apt—we worldly folk—to think that
no woman becomes a nun, unless she has had some
bitter disappointment in love, or seeks to do penance
for wordly error, or to escape from sorrow or suffering.
Sister Annunciata sought the religious life for none
of these reasons. She had enjoyed a happy, careless
girlhood, the world had offered her no trials; the
pleasures of youth were open to her, as were the joys
of happy womanhood. But her sensibilities were not
yet awakened, she had never known what love meant,
though she had been sought in marriage. So the
ordinary social gaieties took but slight hold upon her,
and life meant nothing to her but home affections and
a passion for the arts.

But one day she saw a strong man suddenly smitten

with paralysis, and she realised all at once the littleness of life, and how it should be used, such as it is,
as a preparation for a greater.   Then all her religious
tendencies developed, and she bethought her how to
make her life most useful while she was striving for
Divine grace.   To devote herself entirely to prayer,
as many sisterhoods do, seemed to her selfish, and so,
while she elected to renounce the world for the sake
of her own soul, she felt that she could use such gifts
and knowledge as she possessed for the instruction
of the youth of her own sex, who sought the educational influence of the convent.   Therefore, with the
enthusiasm of a lofty purpose she entered upon
her novitiate, and then, after two years, as no one
questioned her vocation for the religious life, she
took the final irrevocable vows that severed her from
home and from the world.   Her life as a novice had
been made smooth for her, and all had endeavoured
to show her the alluring side of the religious life, and
strengthen her in the sense of duty that impelled her
to adopt it.   But no one warned her of the arduous
life of self-suppression that was before her : no one
told her that she was actually more fitted for the
world than the cloister ; that the sensibilities still

dormant in her might some day awaken, when too late to be warmed with the human sympathy that they needed, and then be frozen in her heart, after much pain. So when I knew Sister Annunciata she had lived "unspotted from the world" some ten years or so, and had brought herself seemingly into a spirit of sublime submissiveness.

But had she not suffered terrible affliction of the soul during those years? For her spirit was proud and sensitive, and in small and narrow communities there are small and narrow jealousies, and authority is sometimes tyrannical. But Sister Annunciata is a woman of iron will and indomitable self-command, while she makes the light of faith the only beacon of her life. Therefore she has schooled herself to accept every cross with equanimity, while the natural cheerfulness of her disposition enables her to seem content and happy, as well as to inspire happiness in others.

Many were the talks I had with Sister Annunciata as we wandered over the grassy slopes and through the groves and gardens of the convent; and though the unusual circumstances may have appealed strongly to my imagination, certainly converse with woman never filled me with deeper and keener interest. Her vivacious and sympathetic personality and her renunciation of the world seemed so utterly at variance. She would evince the liveliest interest in worldly affairs, and encourage me to tell her of the men and women who are doing the work of the world, of my own personal friends, of my own feelings, of my mundane interests, and she would discuss all these with me, on sufferance as it were, and then remind herself every now and then, by religious allusions, that her life was utterly apart from mine.

She would love me to talk of poetry and romance, and, somehow or other, we would generally drift thence to religious mysticisms and the problems of life and death, which she would always solve with the logic of faith, and beg me not to try and prove her wrong. Talking to her was not like talking to other women; she could draw my soul out as by some enchantment, and the poetry of the place and its surroundings seemed to weave a spell about me. In her presence my ordinary life seemed so far away, and I suppose she was quite a woman, but to me she appeared always a kind of dream-woman. I never could quite associate her with her surroundings, and yet I could never imagine her

anywhere else. It was so incongruous to think of her
bright mind being shut away from society, yet she
seemed to belong to that grey stone building and the
wooded slopes with the sea beyond.

But Sister Annunciata is so different from all the
other nuns. Her mental capacity is so much greater
that she is not bound by the narrow prejudices of the
others, which accounts for her greater sway over the
minds and affections of her pupils. But then, perhaps,
her Sisters are happier than she is, for all her cheerfulness and her laughter; not that she would ever own
that she was not happy, though perhaps she would
allow you to use the term "content" in preference.
Content she is by reason of her will, and peace she
has by reason of her faith and the place; but happiness is not the result of volition, it is an expression of
the soul acted upon from without. But Sister Annunciata cannot be happy so easily as the other Sisters,
for her soul, being larger and more active, requires
more to make it happy; while the Reverend Mother,
who has been half a century "in religion," is as happy
as she can imagine it possible to be, so long as she can
pray to her heart's content, and tell her beads in the
sunshine. She can conceive no one reading any

I

poetry but that which piously sings the praises of the
Saints, and would probably cast up her eyes in horror
did she know that Sister Annunciata had ever read
Shelley.

"I don't care to know what they do in the world,"
said the old nun to me, when I marvelled that she knew
nothing of the worldly events of the day, "we are
much happier as we are." And, after all, it is only habit
that makes us crave for news. If I lived far away
from the busy hum of men, amid such peace and
beauty, I think I should soon grow accustomed to eat
my breakfast without the accompaniment of a morning
paper. It is possible to school oneself to anything,
at least, so I have learnt from my visits to that convent and my friendship with Sister Annunciata, though
doubtless a great deal of purposeless self-sacrifice is
endured for mistaken enthusiasm.

I wonder if Sister Annunciata would have been
happier had she not renounced the world, but pursued
a sphere of usefulness outside the convent. Perhaps
not, after all. Anyhow, her beloved pupils would
not have been so happy, for she is their idol. And
maybe when, in the little convent chapel, she pours out
her virgin soul in solemn organ strains, or when she

communes alone with Nature in those sweet, silent groves, and sends her dreams of higher life across the lovely landscape, she knows more peace than could ever have been hers amid the fever and fret of the toiling world of men.

THE CHEERY WOMAN

EVERY one loves Mrs. Merrysmile, she is so bright
and cheery and lovable, in a holiday way. To be
with her is as good as going to the seaside, her breezy
talk being as so much ozone. Yes, she is very popular;
a kind of female Brighton, that one goes to for the
purpose of being mentally braced up with general
cheeriness and gaiety and excitement. Other women
are our Cromers and our Birchingtons, whither we
go for soothing rest and idle dreaming and world-
forgetting but Mrs. Merrysmile is our London-by-the-
Sea. We dress ourselves in our best to please her,
and she keeps us on the alert. If we be dull and out

of sorts, she takes it as a personal reproach, for she
is so cheery herself that she cannot understand any
ailment or misfortune being sufficiently depressing to
counteract her influence. In her eyes dulness is an
unpardonable offence, while to be invalided is to
incur her serious displeasure ; if you chance to be
either, Mrs. Merrysmile attributes it merely to temper.
She will tell you with a charmingly frank affectation
that she hates the afflicted, and that the positively
poor revolt her ; but she professes to entertain the
greatest sympathy with enterprising criminals, while the
audaciously unscrupulous bankrupt is actually a hero
in her eyes —a contrariness which must not be regarded
as due to any flaw in her moral attitude, for that is
quite above reproach, but simply to that effervescent
cheeriness which will not accept defeat in any form.
She cannot understand any one being beaten by
circumstances, for, as she rather illogically puts it,
"Circumstances were made for slaves ; I make my
own." She says a great many things like this, by the
way, and convinces herself, at all events, even if others
fail to quite catch her meaning.

She is a masterful little woman, and among her own
relations and immediate friends she is a perfect

autocrat. Her constant cheeriness commands everything, and preserves a family unity, for in every emer-
gency, in any dispute, in any trouble, Mrs. Merrysmile
is the centre towards which they all make, from
which radiates all the harmony. How many a family
quarrel has been averted by her happily apposite wit,
how many a cloud has she laughed away with the sunshine of her cheerful little heart! For though she
pretends that humour rather than affection is the key-
note of her life, that she would sacrifice any tender
sentiment for the sake of a joke, Mrs. Merrysmile is
brimming over with love of kith and kind, and is
peculiarly sensitive to that touch of nature which
makes the whole world kin. Her never-failing cheeriness enables her to find some subject of interest everywhere, and the most commonplace stranger has some
point that will appeal to her. Her universal sympathy
is, in fact, quite remarkable. She can talk with equal
interest to the washerwoman with seventeen children,
a drunken husband and the rheumatics, and to the
lady-novelist with a few published books and an
inordinate idea of their merits and her own fame. She
will enter into discussion upon any subject of interest
to the person with whom she may chance to be

conversing, irrespective of possibly her complete ignorance of it, yet somehow she will leave an impression that she is quite conversant with the matter. Her cheery manner and happy knack of saying the right thing at the right moment would, I believe, carry her triumphantly through a debate at the Royal Society, while I am convinced that if she had a seat in Parliament, the members below the gangway would accept her as their leader. They would not elect her ; she would simply assume the position as a matter of course, and there would be an end of the matter, of course. Some women are born to lead as some men are, and whatever the circumstances of their lives, they will lead those around them. Mrs. Merrysmile is decidedly one of these women, but she leads by her perpetual, irrepressible cheeriness. There is no gainsaying it, it carries you along like a flood.

When I first met Mrs. Merrysmile I was in a hopeless state of depression. I had been disappointed by a woman I loved, and was very miserable, though I have no doubt I thoroughly deserved my fate. The fact is, when I was in love I was so heart-whole about the matter, it became so absolutely the only part of my life with which I had any concern, that I am now quite convinced I must have been a nuisance to the object of my adoration. For women do not love like this; they do not care to be perpetually in the society of their lover, they want change and the liberty of the subject. But, to a man who has no confidence in himself, that liberty of the subject, in the case of the woman he loves, always suggests possibilities of being superseded by some more engaging lover. Women are not as constant as men. I say this in no reproachful spirit, it is simply that their keener sensibility renders them more liable to receive fresh impressions, and to feel the influences of new personalities. Therefore, to a self-suspecting lover as I have always been, doubting my own powers to engage a woman's constancy, jealousy, with all its petty irritations and its trivial tyrannies, was bound to come between her and myself. It needs a very strong and deep love to accept jealousy as an every-day accompaniment, and I do not suppose I was able to inspire that. So my love-dreams were roughly interrupted, and I was left to get over my sorrow and disappointment as best I could. Happily for me, Mrs. Merrysmile chanced upon my life at this opportune time. What I should have done without her I scarcely dare to think. Anyhow, some years have passed since then, and life has still its possibilities.

I remember, at our first meeting, in answer to some remark of hers, I said, " Nothing matters," and she reproved me with, " Everything matters." From that moment her cheeriness began to exert its influence upon my life, for she had immediately divined that something was wrong with me, and she determined to set it right. With a woman's instinct she guessed it was love. A man would have put it down to liver; but a woman is sure that love is at the root of all evil. So Mrs. Merrysmile began to work in her own cheery, womanly way, and I, little suspecting her methods, lent myself to them entirely. She would draw me out every day on the subject of my love, and I, believing her to be wholly sympathetic, would tell her all that was in my heart, and she would say that she liked me to talk of that other woman. And I would do so, until, without noticing it, I talked less of her, and found that I was drifting into an interest for Mrs. Merrysmile herself, irrespective of her sympathy in my love affair. Then this became accentuated by her persistent high spirits and jocularity, for though our surroundings of sea and cliff and cornfields, with

the infinite poetry of ever-changing skies and moonlit
nights, with their majestic mysteries, held me ever in
the sentimental mood, and I believed her to be in
tune with me, I would frequently receive a shock of
discord from her sudden and unconscious leap from
the sentimental to the grotesque, from the sublime to
the ridiculous.   She would rudely break an exquisite
silence, which to me had meant a meeting of souls, a
mute embrace of thoughts, with some irrelevant remark, some inconsequent gossip, which would jar
upon me terribly, but which would really bring me
nearer to her, for I would obstinately refuse to believe
I had mistaken her soulfulness and beautiful womanliness, notwithstanding those jarring inconsistencies,
which I could only regard as the excrescences of her
natural cheeriness.

So I grew to love her in spite of myself, and then I
began to realise that Mrs. Merrysmile was really an
agreeable little flirt who had only taken any trouble
to cultivate my affection—which she certainly did very
artistically—because I was so absorbed in the woman
who had naturally grown tired of me.   This, to Mrs.
Merrysmile, seemed not only a great pity for myself,
but a slight to her own vanity, a waste of sound affection,

and to remedy it presented an interesting experiment for a few idle weeks' occupation. Those silences which I thought so beautifully mutual in feeling, as we sat and gazed over the blue deep, and into those wonderful summer skies which seemed to contain a world's epic in their spacious mysteries, were, after all, most humorous interludes to her, full of amusing conjecture; but she could no more help all this than she could help talking.

Life is a constant carnival to Mrs. Merrysmile, and love is a delightful pastime which is necessary for her entertainment. There is no harm in it; her love-making is, indeed, of the most innocent kind, in fact, it is purely psychological, without a suspicion of passion, which would only seem incongruous to her. To be loved is essential to her; every one who comes in contact with her must give her of his heart's best affection. She is satisfied with nothing else, and though she and her husband are on terms of mutual affection and perfect confidence, she takes all the love she can get as her absolute right. That she should give any in return never occurs to her; it is sufficient that she scatters her cheeriness broadcast, relieves her friends and relations of all their depressions, keeps them in good spirits, and, if they be dull or ill, bullies them with a view to mending their ways. But she loves, in her own way, as the butterfly loves the flower that it casually kisses in the garden, and surely the flower is all the sweeter for the butterfly's kiss. I know I feel all the better for having touched hearts with Mrs. Merrysmile, though her way of loving was not my way, and my sentimental devotion was as congruous with her butterfly heart-flutterings as the Nasmyth steam-hammer with the tin-tack.

The humour of the situation was always uppermost in her mind though it had to compete for this place with the gratification of her vanity and the pleasure of passing the time cheerfully for us both, and she could not understand that the whole affair did not present itself to me in exactly the same light. As immunity from contradiction of any kind had been hers throughout her life, both as maid and as wife, my frequent failure to fall in with her ideas as to the humour of our flirtation - for to her it was really nothing more, though in her innocent way she pretended to regard it as a real love-affair—it was not to be wondered at that our confidential communings became less constant, until my lover-like attitude developed into that of the

elderly friend. You cannot go on loving desperately
a woman to whom everything is simply funny, or, at
least, suggestion for a jest. And that is one of the
drawbacks of a *par excellence* cheery woman. You
want to love the woman rather than her jokes, or even
her bright spirits, charming as the faculty for these
undoubtedly is. But as a man's moods vary so does
he expect the woman he loves to respond to them. In-
cessant cheeriness and readiness to see only the quaint
or comic side of things, if unchecked in expression,
is apt to turn life into a farce, and even the merriest
farce jars when one is only in the temper for romantic
drama, or when pathos is the dominant note of the
moment.

Yet with all her irresponsibility of feeling, with all
her irrelevance of mood, Mrs. Merrysmile is quite one
of the most delightful companions for man or woman.
She is a woman's woman quite as much as a man's,
but I would specially recommend her at times of joy
and frolic rather than of sorrow—however excellent
her intention to cheer you and help you make the
best of everything. For so casual is her nature that
troubles will scarcely present their actual aspect to her
in relation to all the surrounding facts of life ; she will

think they are not really as heavy and important as
you think them, but rather chide you for making such
a fuss.   It is from no lack of sympathy that this
charming little woman will not always understand your
feelings, but simply that her native cheerfulness is so
superabundant; she cannot realise that things can
ever be as bad as less optimistic persons imagine.   And
if, when you feel ill, she tells you bluntly that there
is little or nothing the matter with you, it is only
because she believes too much sympathy is not conducive to effort towards recovery, and she hates to see
people ill.   It is perhaps very irritating, but it is her
way, and it is quite good-natured.

I should hardly recommend Mrs. Merrysmile as a
consoler in a house of mourning; the very brightness
of her disposition might clash with the grief of the
bereaved ones, and an obstinate contrariness of spirit,
coupled with a desire to make everybody as cheerful
as herself, might, perhaps, give pain where she intended comfort.   Nor would Mrs. Merrysmile be a
suitable wife for a man of melancholy mood or morose
temper, for she would jar upon him with her intemperate cheerfulness and unmuzzled mirth, while he
would bore her unutterably.   But she is just happily

placed as she is, with a husband ready to worship the
ground she walks upon, with a host of friends and
relations that defer to her autocratic word with infinite
pleasure, and a friend, who is glad to have loved her,
but is just as content, and after all, perhaps happier,
to have won her friendship through the more subtle
and intimate insight into her nature gained as a lover.
She is a delightful little creature, but she should
always live in the sunshine and amid the roses.
There she is perfectly appropriate, and life is the richer
and the fairer for her presence.

LADY GLADYS PARCHMENT is one of the most familiar, as she is one of the most admired, figures in London society, and to the ordinary observer she is one of the most happy and fortunate. For is she not exceedingly beautiful? Does she not come of an old and noble family, though it be more distinguished in these hard times for pedigree and nobility, perhaps, than for property? And is she not wedded to a man of splendid fortune and reputation? True he is some twenty years her senior; but then, if he were not, he would hardly be of sufficiently mature age to have attained the dignity of a judgeship, and in this intensely practical age we are obliged to pay a price for everything. In her case, Lady Gladys, the daughter of a poor Irish earl, had to pay for the advantage of marrying a wealthy English judge the price of heavy disparity in years, with its consequences. And was Sir Drury Parchment worth the price?

Had Lady Gladys not been born in the purple, so that, by the conventional aspirations of her order, and a kind of fictional duty to her rank and station, she was constrained to make a wealthy marriage or suffer social obscurity, would she not rather have wedded less advantageously, from a worldly point of view, and more congruously in a heart sense? But it is very difficult for a girl—with little experience of the world beyond the ball-room, the tennis-lawn, and the hunting-field, who cannot possibly realise all that matrimony means—to argue successfully against the logic of wealth and position, when her heart remains an unconcerned auditor. Yet marriage either makes or mars the life of the individual it cannot leave it *in statu quo*, but must either complete or disintegrate it. Irrespective of material fortune, the life of a man or woman may be adjudged a success or a failure according as it is blessed with the right mate or cursed with the wrong one. So long as it remains actually mateless, and without the response of love, it is simply unfinished.

Now, when a beautiful and brilliant woman, with

apparently every worldly advantage at her command, takes a pessimistic view of life, and assumes a cynical attitude towards the world, you may be sure that she has married the wrong man, and made a failure of her life. And you cannot converse long and familiarly with Lady Gladys Parchment without perceiving this. Her talk may sparkle with wit, and ripple over with humour, but it will be the keen, biting wit of the cynic, the bitter humour of the pessimist, and there is no mistaking it for the pleasantry of cheerful content. Her sarcasm has a grim laughter in it, but it is as the mocking laughter of disappointed genius when it hears superficial talent winning the popular plaudits. In society Lady Gladys shines because of her personal and mental gifts, she loves society simply for the enjoyment of conquest which it affords, and this has to make up for so much else in her life. Indeed, she finds so little else in life at all.

Sir Drury Parchment is a man of violent temper and dyspeptic temperament, but his moods are various, inconsequent, and unexpected. It is impossible to foresee the changes of his temper. He will sulk for days without any apparent cause, he will, for weeks

together, exhibit no interest whatever in the doings of
his wife and child, and then suddenly he will evince
a fierce jealousy of every
detail that concerns them,
but this will never be
accompanied by any
show of affection. Sen-
timent of any kind is
foreign to his nature, and,
whatever his mood, it is
always pure egotism that
dominates it. How such a
confirmed egotist came to

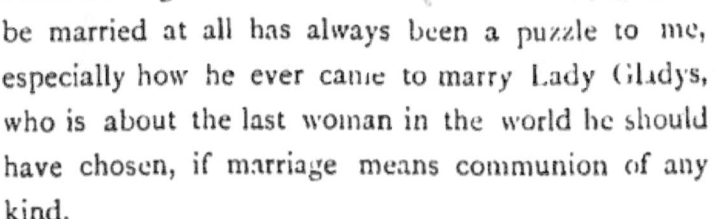

be married at all has always been a puzzle to me,
especially how he ever came to marry Lady Gladys,
who is about the last woman in the world he should
have chosen, if marriage means communion of any
kind.

Lady Gladys always had exceptional intellectual
gifts and a singularly quick comprehension. She would,
even as a girl, swoop down upon a subject and
illuminate it with brilliant paradox which, if not con-
vincing, would certainly be memorable. She would
sum up a character in a few epigrammatic phrases,

and, though the result might be a caricature, it was
certainly a striking one.   She would present an original
view of any subject she discussed, and, though it might
be a view which logical argument could easily prove
fallacious, it would nevertheless leave a distinct personal impression.   For Lady Gladys had the quality of
imagination very strongly, and this coloured her talk
as it mystified her life.   She would never see life and
things and people as they really were.

Sir Drury was struck by her mental faculties; her
sparkling talk amused and interested him as her
beauty delighted him.   He was a widower, and did
not regret the loss of his late wife, whose perpetual
placidity and devoted docility had irritated him more
than any contradiction.   Now he decided that Lady
Gladys should tempt him to a second venture in
matrimony, so he proposed and was accepted; for,
though there was no question of love in the matter, he
was an exceedingly clever as well as wealthy and professionally distinguished man, and he interested her.
She was flattered by his consideration, and she
imagined a future of social triumph for them both.

But marriage soon proved to them that they were
eternally separate, that under no circumstances could

there be any compromise between them. She conceived a loathing towards him from their marriage-day, and he was not slow to perceive this and to resent it. Her very beauty and brilliancy became hateful to him, because he felt that they were not really his, and yet he wished to be master of them. He was jealous that others should admire her, and he have no pride of possession, though she bore his name. So, though they lived before the world according to social conventions, he exercised a species of petty tyranny over her with a view to humiliating her before the society for which she lived, and so spiting her. He would allow her to go entirely her own way for some time, never caring whither she went, never accompanying her in public, never appearing when she "received" at home. Then, of course, people would begin to wonder and whisper, and in defiance she would go out alone all the more, and send out invitations to "At Homes" and dinner-parties, when she would always receive her guests with fictitious apologies for her husband.

But on one occasion, as the guests drove up to the door, they were told by the servants that Lady Gladys could not receive them. No excuse was given, and every one went away wondering. Sir Drury had ordered it so; but this was the crisis. He had humiliated his wife, not only before her friends, but before her servants. How could she continue to live under the same roof with him, to even pretend amicable relations with him! She must go and live elsewhere, and take her child with her. No, that he would not permit. *She* might go where she liked, but the child must remain. So, of course, she remained; for, though she hated her husband more than ever, and now he watched her with jealous suspicion, she was a mother, and the ties of motherhood proved stronger than her conjugal repulsion.

And now her woman's nature asserted itself. Her unfortunate marriage had kept the voices of love and passion till now dumb within her; but in her un-happiness they cried out in sad yearning tones. Her soul ached for true companionship, her womanhood craved for love. Her imagination had hitherto served her, and Society had furnished her with excitement, but now she wanted more, and with the demand came the supply. In fact, there was always a supply of lovers ready to her hand, had she wanted them, for she was beautiful; but she never did want them, though she would accept the constant escort of cavaliers in the Row, to the theatre, and elsewhere.

But these Guardsmen and men-of-fashion who would ride and drive with her, meant nothing to her beyond pleasant riding and driving escorts, and when they tried to be something more—which was not infrequent, considering her personal charms—she laughed it off with amiable sarcasm. One, however, at length appeared in her social circle who drew her to him magnetically. He was not one of the usual Society and club loungers, but a man who had lived a life of adventure in many lands, had seen many strange and wonderful sights, and known many remarkable people. He had explored unknown countries, and contributed new facts to knowledge, so that his name was honoured by learned societies. Yet there was no assumption of the hero about him; on the contrary, there was nothing he so genuinely disliked as being lionised. He was cosmopolitan in ideas, simple and graceful in manner, with a persuasive charm that was almost invincible. He was a born leader of men, had he chosen to lead them; he was a born wooer of women, and he did choose to woo them, for his weakness was a pretty face. But his method of wooing was very insidious. He did not worship at their feet, nor did he play much upon sentiment, but he would mock them with adoration, persuasively find fault with them, cunningly coax them into defending themselves and their sex against charges of inconstancy, frivolity, and frailty, and then perplex them with paradox and sophistry, until they were quite convinced that he was the most fascinatingly dangerous man they had ever met, and were simply mad to meet him again. Then he would make himself scarce.

He was just the man to interest Lady Gladys in her unhappy frame of mind; he was so different from all the other men about her. His cosmopolitan cynicism was so refreshing to her, his sophistry so seductive. She also, in her turn, interested him much, for there was no doubt she had brains. Women to him were usually more or less of toys, but Lady Gladys was an intellectual being, she exercised his mental fencing powers, and was difficult wooing. He hated Society, it was too silly to amuse him, but he was obliged to endure it for the sake of Lady Gladys. He meant to be her lover, so he allowed her to procure him invitations to a series of "at homes," where he should meet her. He would attend her daily in the Park,

he would drop in every afternoon at teatime, and if
she was going to the theatre, he would, of course, have
a stall next to hers. And all the while this love-
making was prosecuted with masterly tactics, and she
was falling deeply in love with him. She had never
known love in her life before, and now it filled her
life, and made it tolerable. What her lover lacked
in emotional delicacies and sentimental refinements,
she supplied out of her own imagination, and was not
aware that he lacked them; and she was compara-
tively happy, and cared little or nothing for her husband's petty tyrannies. She was becoming hardened
to them — and had not she now a lover as well as
her child to love? After all, love makes up the sum
of our lives; it is the only thing we cannot miss without being wretched. Lady Gladys had had everything
else till now, and now she loved and believed herself
loved. Might she not be happy in spite of Sir Drury?
Though she was tied to him for life, what happiness
had he ever given her?

But now people began to busy themselves with
gossip about Lady Gladys, to wonder how long it
would be before Sir Drury woke up to the state of
affairs. It was only a whisper here and there, of

course; but still it was a whisper, and even whispers
are sometimes heard by those not intended to hear.
So Sir Drury heard, not that he had not known
before; but it was only the whisper that gave him
a weapon to strike with.   She loathed him; she had
told him so more than once; then she should not
love another.

So when her lover called as usual one day, he was
told that Lady Gladys could not receive him, but
that Sir Drury would be glad to see him in his study;
and then the cold-blooded old judge told him of the
whisper, and left it to him to discontinue his visits.
Lady Gladys waited long for her lover that day, and
when she heard at length that he had come and gone,
she was furiously indignant.   Of course, he felt bound
in honour to give her the option of running away with
him, but he was not sorry when she refused on account
of her child.   "She would only have run away with
some one else later on," was the reflection with which
he cynically consoled himself.

And now I often wonder, when I see the chilling
scorn with which Lady Gladys and Sir Drury treat
one another, whether she ever regrets not having
taken that step which might possibly have given her

happiness, and certainly cost her her social status; but when I see her fondling her curly-haired little boy, I feel sure she does not regret it. But she is more cynical than ever; her faith in man and woman, love and the world, is hopelessly shaken. She is a confirmed pessimist, because conjugal happiness has been unknown to her.

MRS. RESTLESS I shall call her. Not that she would object to my proclaiming her actual identity. In fact, I think she would prefer it, for she loves to be talked about ; and, as for seeing her name in print, I fancy she would do much for the privilege, and then carefully cut out the page for the edification of her friends, and wonder how she had obtained, not merited, such publicity. Not merited, because she will confess to knowing all about that. Who but she does so much for everybody? Who is so active in every matter of public interest? Then why should not she deserve newspaper recognition, as much as Mrs. Montmorency Dazzle or Lady Capel-Courtney, who only occupy their time in the frivolous amusements of Society, and employ expensive dressmakers to win them paragraphs by making them "look weil" in the fashionable material of the moment?

This is a sore point with little Mrs. Restless, for she really believes that her continuous occupiedness, in spite of the vast amount of nothing she achieves, is of infinite value to the community at large, and her own personal acquaintances in particular, whereas Mrs. Dazzle is of no use to any one, except as an ornament for the ball-room, and a walking advertisement for her costumier. These are Mrs. Restless's views, and she has very strong views on every subject, though perhaps they would not amount to much if subjected to the slightest analysis. . But she does not know that ; for she is always too busy to analyse anything. She is a woman of action, she will tell you ; she must always "be up and doing." And so she wastes a great deal of valuable time which might otherwise be devoted to idling that is worth living for, that is full of pleasurable suggestion, instead of commonplace and pretentious time-frittering ; busy-idleness, in fact, which is neither the one thing nor the other, neither good idling nor good business.

Women seldom idle well ; they do not understand the art. They make it too much of a business, and so miss the spirit of true idling. Now I reckon myself something of a *connoisseur* in this matter, for if

there be one art with which I am familiar in all its
branches, and on terms of perfect understanding, it is
this art of idling.   A fine art, look you, that must be
studied with the same assiduity and sympathy as paint-
ing, poetry, music, love-making, lying, or any other of
those accomplishments that have been reckoned
among the fine arts.   Your
true idler is born, not made,
but in the easy and happy
evasion of work and
its responsibilities he
proves himself the
artist. The obli-
gation to effort
is a necessity
to him, but his art
teaches him how to make a virtue of necessity by
shunting the obligation on to pleasanter lines, while
the effort fails naturally upon other shoulders which
perhaps ought to bear it for some penance they have
no doubt deserved.   At least, your idler consoles
himself so, if he concern himself at all about the
matter.   Thus, to idle artistically is not to vulgarly
waste time, but to adorn it as with May-day garlands.

And every one who cultivates this most delightful of arts may build himself a Castle of Pleasaunce in the midst of this workaday world, wherein he may joyously live at ease, and listen to the hearty songs of the toilers, who have never dreamed of Arcady, and who know nought but that each hour must produce its full profit of work.

But to return to Mrs. Restless. She is the busy-idle woman *par excellence*. To idle simply is impossible to her ; she must always be indefinitely busy with definite results. There is seldom any uncertainty about the results, generally they are practically valueless, or not worth the trouble they have cost, but they occupy a great deal of time in achieving for all that. She will take up some charitable object, and go from place to place and worry all her friends and acquaintances in the cause, and at the end of her efforts she will find that, had she at first given a certain reasonable sum from her own pocket, she would not only have come off cheaper than she has by frittering out small payments, but she would have saved much trouble and time, which might have been more advantageously employed. If she plans any pleasure, she will, instead of enjoying it in the right, rational manner of the true idler, make so much fuss about it, and expend so much argument upon it, that it becomes a business and loses all semblance of pleasure.

Figuratively speaking, Mrs. Restless is in a chronic state of moral perspiration; effort oozes out of every pore of her being. She does not understand repose, but rather seems to have discovered the secret of perpetual motion. She cannot sit still. If in her drawing-room you be calmly and comfortably ensconced in a luxurious arm-chair, from which you feel convinced that wild horses would be powerless to drag you, Mrs. Restless will enter, dusting the back of a chair, or changing the position of some trivial ornament as she approaches. Then when you think she is actually settled for conversation, she will rise to rearrange an antimacassar at the further end of the room, and probably insist upon your assisting her to move the piano.

At the breakfast-table Mrs. Restless is very trying, for she will never allow a plate or dish, or any eating utensil, to remain in the position into which it naturally falls in the course of the meal. She plays therefore a perpetual game of draughts with the breakfast things. I remember on one occasion watching an amusing game. Mrs. Restless was discussing some philanthropic plan—she is nothing if not philanthropic—with an old gentleman, whose constant habit as he talked was to push everything by degrees into the middle of the table ; but Mrs. Restless could not stand that, so she as persistently pushed everything back again, thus giving fresh play to the old gentleman's idle fingers, while she was kept constantly occupied at this purpose-less business. And this is typical of all that Mrs. Restless does.

If she goes into the garden, and you invite her to the tempting repose of a hammock which hangs under sun-shading boughs, or of a long wicker-chair which, surrounded by rose-trees, suggests the " idle dreaming of an empty day," and into which, but for politeness sake, you would fain have flung yourself, will she enjoy the proffered luxuries of lounging restfulness? Not a bit of it. She cannot waste the opportunity of plucking dead leaves from the flower-bushes, sweeping fallen leaves from the gravel paths—all the gardener's actual business. Heavens! you expect her next to take a duster and flip off all the casual dust from the trees, or dry the dew from the flowers. And meanwhile you have self-denyingly taken the less comfortable lounge,

L.

leaving the place of perfect repose vacant for this busy-idle woman, who will not enjoy it.

Mrs. Restless scorns the unintellectual and despises the frivolous. She believes herself to be the reverse of both, and entertains great opinions of her own mental powers. But, dear thing, she is naïvely superficial; she has, unfortunately, no time for reading, and—thank goodness !—she has no logic. If she had she would be unendurable, for she would wish to reason out her aggressive busying. Of course she firmly believes she is logical. What woman does not, and would not be offended if you hinted to the contrary? But, truly, a logical woman loses half the charm of her sex, for her moods must be consequent and responsible. Now, Mrs. Restless redeems much of her irritating faculty of idle occupation by her delightfully amusing inconseqence, of which, however, she is quite seriously unconscious. She will go off at a tangent without any provocation, which to the humorously inclined outsider frequently provides food for mirth, though to Mr. Restless the fact of not knowing what his wife's irresponsible energy will prompt her to say and do next must be somewhat temper-trying. Nevertheless, he adores her, and when he is not reproving

her in his practical way, while she attempts to argue
his utter incapacity to understand her high-minded
aims, they do a good deal of billing and cooing,
though she is always too restless to enjoy even the
repose of the melting, affectionate mood for many
minutes together.

If her husband, to whom she is devotedly attached,
comes home tired from his daily work, and inclined to
rest in the society of his wife, she will fret him with
the petty details of her day's doings, of which he will
not find much to approve, seeing that her "much ado
about nothing" has perhaps involved the departure of a
valuable servant, the estrangement of a useful acquaintance, or a quarrel with an excellent tradesman. Then
she will have muddled up her engagements so that
she is obliged to drag her unwilling husband from
the much-needed quiet of his domestic hearth to some
purposeless party, where boredom is inevitable.

In spite of her professed dislike to the idle members of the community, of the Society butterflies that
flutter over the flowered fields of pleasure, Mrs. Restless is never happier than when she is going to parties,
and theatres, and fêtes; but when she does so she
speaks of it as a duty rather than an amusement, and

grumbles that Society keeps her so busy. Not that she allows social occupations to interfere with her domestic cares. She has children, and they know it; and servants, and *they* know it. She never allows them to forget that they are *her* children and *her* servants. Not a detail concerning either escapes her, but she misses the general harmony in effect. She worries about everything and everybody, until I verily believe the infant in the cradle longs to find prussic acid in its bottle, if only to obtain a little peace.

And yet there is a great deal of good nature and fine feeling in Mrs. Restless, and half of her idle industry is due to her over-heartedness and her concern for the pleasure and welfare of others, coupled with an instinctive feeling of economy. She will spend a whole day and worry all her propinquious friends and relations in her endeavours to give away a ticket that has been sent to her for some theatrical or musical entertainment, in order that it shall not be wasted. "Somebody will be glad of it," she thinks, and so any sacrifice of time and trouble must be made to find out *who* will. Kindness and generosity are at the bottom of most of her actions, but there is too much of the vexatious atmosphere of wasted energy and frittered time. She will take an infinite amount of trouble for an infinitely small result, and invariably in the interests of others; yet her genuine friends sincerely like her, and her relations are fond of her, though they laugh at her follies, and amiably ridicule her untimely and misplaced energies and her magnificent muddling. Her children love her, though she wearies them with over-carefulness and excessive attention; and her husband, on the whole, thinks himself a very fortunate individual, though he certainly would be content if his wife were a little less busy and a little more idle. There would then, perhaps, be more calm and comfort in his home.

On the whole, I feel that I frankly do not bear Mrs. Restless any grudge for not having fallen in with my matrimonial views years ago, when we were both in our teens, and I used to regard her enthusiasm about everything, and her ardent activity in the cause of, Heaven knows what, as something approaching the divine. And now I call it busy-idleness! Well, the illusions of youth give place to the illusions of age; but happily we have illusions always. Life would be terribly dull without them.

Mrs. Restless is, beyond a doubt, an excellent wife, as in the long ago of my boyhood I thought she would be; but I am glad she is another's.

THE SKITTISH OLD MAID

I BELIEVE I may consider myself a passably amiable man, and I could certainly produce ample testimony to prove I am so considered by a large variety of impartial witnesses, ranging from my baby nieces to my septuagenarian mother, and not forgetting to include my tailor. I am of equable temper, and charitably expansive in matters of opinion. I generally contrive to find excuses for the foibles and failings of my fellow-creatures, and, had I but the gift of oratory, I believe I could melt any jury to mercy, where an ordinary professional advocate for the defence would only aggravate a conviction. I am forgiving to a fault, and hence, if Pope's dictum on the humanity of error and the divinity of forgiveness count for truth, I must surely have in me some kinship with the gods. But though I can so charitably temper my mind as to frequently regard murder from the criminal's point of view as justifiable homicide, forgery and embezzlement as a practical protest in favour of socialism, and arson as a mere tribute to the picturesque, there is one crime I can never bring myself to contemplate with any toleration. When one person commits boredom upon another, he puts himself beyond the pale of mercy. I am an amiable man, but I cannot bear to be bored.

Now, there is a class of persons who seem to have come into the world for no other purpose than to test the patience of others. To this class Miss Kittenish most undoubtedly belongs. I cannot determine any other plausible reason for her existence. I have thought that her constant devotion to her invalid mother might have had something to do with it, her usefulness in directing the domestic affairs of the household, her eager interest in the concerns of her five unmarried sisters, her exemplary energy in parish mission-work, or her active enthusiasm in the matter of school-treats; but, praiseworthy as all this is, I can scarcely regard all or any one of these causes as the *raison d'être* of Miss Kittenish. She was born to be a bore, to try the temper of the amiable, to prove that we are all mortal, even the most charitable.

Bores are of two kinds — active and passive. The

active are the worse, and in that category Miss Kittenish must be placed, her special aggravation being that she is so playful, and has a passion for parlour-games—a very virulent form of boredom to practise upon the amiable person. Now, be it remembered that Miss Kittenish is a spinster of a very uncertain age—so uncertain, in fact, that there is no telling what childish prank she may not be up to. But that which may be all very well when directing the rollicking festivities of a school-treat is apt to be aggressively out of place in an assembly of grown-up and presumably reasonable persons. Yet that is just what Miss Kittenish is unable to realise. The fascination of the round game seems to have stunted her mental growth, and all her friends suffer in consequence. Heaven knows, no one is more amenable than I to frivolity of any kind; no one is readier to make a fool of himself at the proper season, and under the necessary inspiration. And as for playing with children, no game is too primitive for me, nothing that they can expect me to do is too idiotic, nothing too undignified.

For the nonce I will set a fool's cap upon my dignity, and laugh at it. I will sing, " This is the

way we wash our clothes," and act the attendant
"business," as they call it in stage-parlance, till I go
perfectly hoarse in my throat. I will "hunt the
slipper," or play "puss in the corner," and roll and
romp on the floor with my little friends, and enjoy it
as much as any of them. Let me loose among their
toys, and witness my enthusiasm. Give me tops to
spin, clockwork engines to set running, tin soldiers to
shoot down with spring cannons, or a box of bricks
to work my architectural fancy withal, and you shall
see a transformation to which fairy lore alone can
supply a parallel—you shall see thirty years fly away
and leave me a child of six.

But Miss Kittenish is so playful that she is entirely
unable to discriminate between the amusements of the
very juvenile and the adult; and this is painfully
forced upon one-whenever one is weak enough to
accept an invitation to a social gathering at the Kittenishes', who, I may add, live in the suburbs. This
I do periodically, because they are such old family
friends—they are, indeed, a sort of heirloom from
the last generation, which has to be kept up. It would
sometimes be curious to trace the origin of old family
friends, from the cumbersome heirloom point of view.

How I ever came to incur the obligation of visiting the Kittenishes I do not recollect. I know I was taken there as a child, and I remember that in those days there was a series of maiden aunts similar to the present brood, and I can recall playing games with them to my youthful enjoyment, so that the revived acquaintance has now become a traditional duty. But I am grown-up now, and have been so these many years, and so have Miss Kittenish and her five sisters; but it makes no difference. They invite a number of friends to spend the evening there, all of whom have entered upon the business of life, and consequently are, or should be, interested in the events or social problems of the day. Some may belong to the liberal professions, some may be votaries of the arts, others merely competitors in the race for wealth, or idle killers of time. But will these be permitted to converse under the Kittenish roof on topics which appeal to them? Emphatically, no! Miss Kittenish has taken care to leaven her guests with a few persons of her own mind, and as soon as you are on the point of learning from a Stock Exchange wiseacre whether Egyptian Unifieds are going up or down, or from an omniscient journalist the date of the next Parliamentary dissolution, the name of Tennyson's next poem, the details of Irving's next play, the winner of the next Derby, and the true particulars of the last Cabinet Council, Miss Kittenish approaches you with that diabolically playful expression on her face, which portends " Dumb Crambo " or something equally terrible, and asks you to go out of the room while the rest of the company thinks of something.

I am usually the first victim, being known for an amiable man—how I wish I had cultivated ferocity from my cradle—and after making a feeble defence to the effect that I am so stupid at that kind of thing, I am led away like a lamb to the slaughter. After a few chilly minutes on the landing, during which I vainly contemplate means of escape, I am called back into the room, and find myself in the centre of a circle of presumably intelligent persons waiting to be asked a number of inconsequent questions. All the Kittenish girls are keenly on the alert, but Miss Kittenish is the mistress of the ceremonies; she explains my duties, and I proceed resignedly. Of course I have not the least idea what it is all about, and when, after the dismal proceedings, I am asked to guess the word or proverb or whatever it was, I make a series of random guesses which are so extravagantly absurd that they provoke roars of laughter, and I am voted most amusing —a fatal success.

Miss Kittenish is now all bustle and playfulness, and she once more takes advantage of my amiability, and I am called upon to act in a charade, then to play "Dumb Crambo," and eventually to sit cross-legged upon a broomstick poised upon two chairs, an abominable torture if you succeed, while if you do not, you fall with a sudden bump to the ground. In any case you afford boisterous merriment to the spectators, who are neither on the broomstick nor on the ground. After this my amiability is conquered by my increasing mental depression, aided by the bodily torture involved in the fiendish broomstick trick, and I make all sorts of excuses to elude Miss Kittenish in her fresh devices. She is, however, untiring, and her resource in the matter of parlour-games and tricks is positively amazing. Of course, it is impossible to adopt all her suggestions on a single evening. I diplomatically propose that we should keep some novelties for Christmas; but there is no escape, and, after we are physically wearied by the

more active games, paper and pencils are handed
round, and we are set to play "consequences," then
to write doggerel verses, then to remember as many
towns and countries beginning with G as we can in a
given number of minutes, and other equally aimless
occupations. And what annoys me is that the
majority of sycophantic guests actually encourage
Miss Kittenish in these suburban atrocities, pretending they are amused, while I am doomed to endure
this boredom now and again by family tradition.

If I were not so amiable, I would break from it. I
would never go there again, and then I should be
accused of inconstancy to old friends. This is chain-
ing myself to a sentiment, certainly; but I would
Miss Kittenish were not so playful, or that she con-
fined her volatile spirits to the parish schoolroom, or
the seaside boarding-house, where she is quite an
acquisition and in her element.

To one of these establishments at Eastbourne Miss
Kittenish sometimes accompanies her invalid mother,
and the announcement that " Miss Kittenish is coming" produces as much pleasurable excitement as the
preliminary announcement of a visit from Singer's
Circus to the town of Sleepy Hollow. A vision of

abnormal festivities and something new in parlour-games is immediately conjured up, while it is well known that Miss Kittenish is a perfect mine of conundrums, old and new. For years past she has collected them in manuscript.

But the skittish propensities of Miss Kittenish do not confine themselves to these mild sports. She is of opinion that her personal charms are peculiarly attractive to men, and it is impossible to talk to her without becoming conscious that she is endeavouring to construe your conversation into a flirtation. She really imagines that she is in a chronic state of defence against siege from our sex, and the various ruses of primitive coquetry by which she endeavours to bring on a general engagement are amusing to watch for a little while, though their sameness soon palls. She perpetually asserts her determination never to marry, until one begins naturally to wonder why she finds it necessary to be so emphatic. I believe there is sufficient chivalry still left among us to protect Miss Kittenish from being forced to any step so avowedly repugnant to her feelings. Yet she will take pains to tell you what pretty things this young man said to her, what attention that old man paid her, and to insinuate that

no party is really considered complete unless she graces
it. Her enthusiastic eagerness for entertainment is
perfectly amazing; offer her tickets for anything, and
she will accept them, be it only an amateur theatrical
performance, or a dramatic recital at a local institute.
Of course, if she be the happy possessor of gratuitous
orders for the theatre, she is almost as proud as if she
knew an actor off the stage, which, I need hardly say,
is considered, in suburban circles, a very high distinction.

Miss Kittenish still looks to attain to this, however,
for a friend of the curate's with whom, of course, she
is associated in Sunday-school matters, has promised
to bring to their next social gathering an actor who is
a member of his angling club. Though he is not
perhaps a leading actor, and he still lives domestically
with his wife and children, he did once play "Claude
Melnotte," and is now a low comedian at a West-end
theatre, so that Miss Kittenish will be quite justified
in talking with casual impressiveness of her new
acquaintance, when the introduction is an accomplished
fact. She and her sisters will lionise him, and make
him play games, and expect him to do all sorts of
funny things, so that their friends will go away and tell

everybody how they met Shoppy, the actor, at the
Kittenishes', and how amusing he was, and how he told
them all about " behind the scenes," the way he studied
his own parts and taught all the other actors theirs, and
showed the dramatist how to make his play a success,
the manager how to produce it, and the leading actress
how to act, and then said such clever things about
the injustice of the critics. Miss Kittenish has her
ambitions and her hero-worship, you see, and she
always says that her proper vocation is the stage.
Perhaps she will take to it yet, who knows? She is
for ever volatile, and she never tires of playing charades.

But I often wonder what Miss Kittenish thinks
about when she is alone. She can hardly ask herself
conundrums. Can she really persuade herself that
she is yet young and fascinating? Can she, at her
time of life, find self-delusion so easy? Or does she
know the truth, and realise it in solitude? There must
be an infinite pathos in the lonely meditations of this
skittish old maid, in spite of her invulnerable good
nature. And perhaps, after all, one should look with
charity upon the parlour-games and the conundrums,
for I'm sure Miss Kittenish means well. Nothing
bores *her*.

MRS. MAYFAIR SMARTLY is still a very beautiful
woman; but when I first knew her she was quite
lovely, with all the freshness of youth yet impearled
upon her cheek, and in her eyes a newly-kindled light
of conscious triumph, for her beauty had brought her
fame. From the pretty and petted little wife of a
gallant and good-natured major of dragoons, she
had suddenly become "the beautiful Mrs. Mayfair
Smartly," thanks to the notice of an illustrious personage. Her photographs were in every shop-
window, and no social function was considered complete without her. Admirers swarmed around her
wherever she went; and, when she did not put in an
appearance anywhere, she was nevertheless talked
about--with candour.

Mrs. Mayfair Smartly had been married three or
four years before she became really "somebody."

M

Her husband, Major Mayfair Smartly, was a typical cavalry officer—a tall, well-built man, of the Anglo-Saxon breed, who would lead a forlorn hope or ride a steeplechase with equal readiness and self-possession, a man who loved luxury and ease, but would be dangerous in the face of an enemy. As it happened, however, all his military service had been peaceful, and even in India he had never had the chance of serving on one of the periodical punitive expeditions, for his wife did not let him stay there long enough. She did not like India, it injured her complexion, so she insisted on his exchanging into a regiment at home. He never refused her anything, and, after all, "there is no place like home"; so, having exhausted all the complimentary adjectives of the reporters of the local Indian papers, and furnished as much *gup* for Simla and Calcutta coteries as propriety would permit, pretty Mrs. Mayfair Smartly, accompanied by her husband, bade farewell to Indian society, and sighing for new fields to conquer, made for London.

Major Mayfair Smartly's new regiment was stationed at Aldershot, therefore his wife arranged that she should take an elegant flat in Mayfair, and that he should come up to town constantly, attend her at

any dinners, receptions, or balls to which she might
Le going, and return to Aldershot by the early
morning train
in time for
parade. She
was soon in the
very whirl of
Society, and
her pretty
face and

ready wit were at-
tracting attention ; but   her actual fame
as a beauty dated, I think, from one afternoon at
Hurlingham. She had been presented at the last

drawing-room, and an illustrious personage had made special inquiries about her on account of her good looks. This fact had, of course, reached her, and gladdened her immeasurably, and she was, therefore, in no way surprised when at Hurlingham that afternoon she received a gracious intimation of the Prince's desire to make her acquaintance. The presentation took place in the presence of a representative Society gathering, and for the rest of the afternoon she was honoured of royalty.

After that eventful day, people began to speak of " the new beauty "; the photographers invited her to sit to them, which she did in every instance, and the journalists began to take particular note of her doings, and of her clothes. Henceforth Mrs. Mayfair Smartly was a social notability; her presence could lend distinction to any party, and her custom could make the fortune of any dressmaker, for she knew how to dress.

This may sound trivial and frivolous, but I am not one of those who profess to think lightly of women for paying much attention to their dress. I have invariably found that those women who really understand the art of dress, who know what to wear and

how and when to wear it, possess taste and intelligence
of a more refined order than those who regard costume
in the light of mere clothing, and who not only reveal
no appreciation of a woman's obligation to look her
best at all times, but affect to treat dress altogether as
a subject fit only for the attention of frivolous minds.
Charles Lamb said he hated a man who swallowed his
food affecting not to know what he was eating. He
suspected his taste in higher matters. So, when I
hear a woman-of-the-world say she does not care how
she looks, or what she wears, I feel pretty sure she is
a woman of no taste, in spite of possibly much intellectual pretension, and that she is lacking in personal
charm. When a woman says she leaves her costume
to her dressmaker, I know that she has no mind of
her own, no invention, no resource, no sense of the
fitness of things, and that, however beautiful a gown her
dressmaker may provide her with, she herself is sure
to wear some incongruous hat or cloak, gloves or shoes,
which will disturb the harmony of her appearance,
and so assert her own ignorance.

Now, Mrs. Mayfair Smartly did none of these things;
she was an artist in the matter of attire, and her
personal charm was thereby all the greater. There be

painters, musicians, and poets who may be as daringly
original as they will in their compositions, and yet one
not only feels that they are absolutely right, but that
their innovations must become precedents. So it was
with Mrs. Mayfair Smartly. She could dare to dress
in styles that had not yet received the authority of the
fashion-plates, and so infallibly right was she always
that Fashion was bound to follow her. That Mrs.
Mayfair Smartly wore such a colour, such a material,
or such a design, was sufficient to ensure its general
adoption by those who wished to dress well. In
fashion, therefore, she was a leader rather than a
follower, and, oh, how she was envied while she was
admired.

But Mrs. Mayfair Smartly was not one of those
stolid and superior human beings who can bear success
with equanimity. It intoxicated her. She was "a very
woman," and she loved to be admired. It may have
been very vain on her part, but nothing delighted her
so much as to read or hear praise of her beauty, her
dress, or her talk. She went everywhere, because
wherever she went she won fresh admiration. In
Society everybody knew her, of course, but she would
tire herself to death sooner than miss any reception

where she felt that she might shine, while she would
never miss the Park, the "private views," the opera,
or the fashionable cricket-matches, or race-meetings.
For at these she would always be a centre of attraction,
and people would crowd about her, and those who
knew her not would ask who she was, and those who
knew her would gladly show their knowledge ; and
much admiration would call forth much envious
deprecation, which was a sign of her power, for no
success is won without provoking envy.

But it is not possible to sustain the reputation of a
Society beauty and leader of fashion without much expenditure of money, and, truth to tell, though in comfortable circumstances, Major Mayfair Smartly was by
no means wealthy. What he lacked in wealth, however,
he made up in lavish generosity and devotion to his
wife. He felt that such a beautiful and charming
woman deserved to have her own way in everything ;
and since she had been good enough to marry him,
who had nothing but his good humour and his
stalwart figure, which looked so well in uniform, to
recommend him, the least he could do would be to
give her all she asked. So he began to sell out stock
when her monetary demands far exceeded his income ;

and so by rapid degrees he encroached upon his principal.

But Mrs. Mayfair Smartly, though very practical in the pursuit of pleasure and admiration, was as innocent as a child in the matter of money. She needed it, and her husband supplied it, but it never occurred to her that to pay for the present it was necessary to draw upon the future—that, in fact, her husband's income could not expand in proportion to her extravagances. She lived in a fashionable set, and she was not only bound to do as others did, but her fame as a Society beauty demanded that she should do more. She felt that she needed more dresses, more bonnets, and more diamonds, because she was not plain Mrs. Smartly, but the " beautiful Mrs. Mayfair Smartly." Society expected to see her always in new costumes and she could not disappoint Society. But Mrs. Mayfair Smartly could not dress as she dressed, and live as luxuriantly as she lived, on her husband's income. So she acquired a habit of accumulating debts, and assuming an innocent surprise when the amounts were brought to her notice by requests for immediate payment. And the Major had to begin to borrow money; for he was too good-natured to suggest to his wife that she should moderate her expenditure, and too considerate to trouble her with such a sordid detail as his financial position.

In the meanwhile she went on as usual, the smartest of the smart, appearing in costumes and jewellery which a princess might have envied, driving in a turn-out that an empress would not have scorned, and living as expensively and pleasantly as ever. But kind friends, who knew that the Major was not a millionaire, began to wonder where all the money came from ; and then people began to say unkind things about Mrs. Mayfair Smartly, to couple her name with, not one, but half a dozen wealthy "lords and gentlemen," who were each and all trusty friends of her husband. This was a scandalous shame, for never was woman more impervious to that kind of temptation ; and, after all, Major Mayfair Smartly used to come up from Aldershot nearly every evening, escort his wife to many places, and never interfere with her at any, so that she was really quite fond of him. And a capital fellow he was, except that he erred perhaps on the side of excessive amiability. This it was that brought him to his ruin. He was too amiable, too fond of his wife to take her extravagance in hand, and curb it with a strong rein. Besides, he could spend a pretty penny or two on his own account.

So the crash came at last, and it was quite a surprise to poor Mrs. Mayfair Smartly. She was amazed she could not understand it at all. Why had her husband never told her about it? He treated her like a child, whereas, had he realised that she was a woman, and told her of the financial crisis at hand in their household, she would willingly have made several retrenchments. But now it was too late. Major Mayfair Smartly was obliged to sell out from the army, and sell up the elegant flat in Mayfair. Then he and his wife retired from Society. The beautiful Mrs. Mayfair Smartly no longer figured in the Society journals or the photographers' shop-windows. Worth's knew her no more, and she began to entertain an absolute affection for individual dresses because she wore them – those that she had not sold—so frequently.

They buried themselves in the country, and she tried to convince herself that she liked rural life. He did, because she was part of it to him—all that he knew of it—and he would have liked existence in Timbuctoo if she had only shared it with him. Now,

too, he was relieved of those tiring journeys to Aldershot after balls and receptions, and he had his beloved
wife all to himself.

But Mrs. Mayfair Smartly was not born for country
life, and she felt that she was stagnating. If she
could not live in London, in her old set, she would
make a set for herself; and if the small remnant of
her husband's income would not support them both
in the Metropolis, she must make some money herself.
There are many fields of usefulness and profit open to
ladies nowadays, she would essay one of them. She
knew Society, its ways and persons, why should she
not make use of her knowledge, and become a Society
journalist? Why should she not write racy sketches
of people she had met during her meteoric social
career? Few women knew more of dress than she,
or had more taste ; why should she, then, not employ
her pen to impart some of her ideas upon the gentle
art of dressing well?

It was a happy thought, and Mrs. Mayfair Smartly
has returned to town to regard Society from a new
point of view. She is now the critic instead of the
criticised. The necessity to live has impelled her to
industry, and though she would sooner be spending

her days in luxurious ease, which is really in accordance with her disposition, she devotes herself
assiduously to work. She always had a ready pen,
and now she writes clever stories and articles, and,
continuing to dress fashionably and harmoniously,
though less expensively, she preserves her reputation
as a " smart " woman, though it is now many seasons
since she was the much-talked-about Mrs. Mayfair
Smartly, the beauty of the season.

MRS. HAZARD is a very charming and interesting woman; she is affectionately attached to her husband —a good, amiable, honest man, who denies her nothing; she is the mother of some sweet little children, and the mistress of an elegant household. She entertains a good deal of very congenial society, and every one agrees that she is an admirable hostess, her manners being engaging, and her powers of conversation decidedly above the average, with one specially remarkable quality, the power of concentration. Indeed, Mrs. Hazard has apparently all the domestic and worldly advantages generally regarded as conducive to a woman's happiness; yet she is never content. She is a confirmed gambler, and her life is one of continuous restlessness. The passion for play dominates all her finer feelings, and every other interest becomes subordinate when the excitement of gambling takes possession of her nature.

She is no avaricious person, who is lured to the gaming table by the greed of gain, but she goes there to drain excitement to the dregs, as drunkard's drink brandy. She sets little value on money in the ordinary way, for her husband is in easy circumstances, and can give her all that she can reasonably require for her expenditure, and she spends it freely and with little heed. But money which she stakes upon the turn of a card, the cast of a die, the chances of roulette, or the speed of a race-horse, she hoards like a miser, gathering and seeking to increase her winnings with the avarice of a usurer. She gambles for gambling's sake, and the money is part of the game. It is the excitement of risk and suspense that she craves for, and while she is under its spell she concentrates every intellectual and emotional faculty upon it. Hence, of course, Monte Carlo is her Mecca, and her pilgrimages thither are frequent.

Mrs. Hazard does not take her children with her when she goes to the Riviera. She leaves them at home with her husband, who cannot often absent himself from the

City, and, when he does, prefers salubrious Eastbourne
to seductive Monte Carlo. He hates gambling of all
kinds, he never plays cards or bets, and he rigorously
avoids speculating on the Stock Exchange, although
he is frequently told a "good thing" by his friends
who are "in the swim." That his wife is a gambler,
therefore, is a bitter grief to him, and he watches her
craving for excitement with uneasiness, but, beyond
an occasional persuasive protest, he never reproaches
her. He thinks she will tire of it, but it has become
part of her nature—it will never be eradicated—nor
does her husband quite know how far the passion for
play has absorbed her, or to what extent she indulges
it. As a matter of fact, it has become so necessary to
her, that when she cannot manage to go to Monte
Carlo, she runs over to convenient Boulogne for a day
or two, and there she spends her entire time at the
Casino, at the *Petits Chevaux*, and only leaves the
green table to go into the baccarat room beyond,
where she varies her gambling excitement. She is
generally a lucky player, but even when she loses she
is just as intense in her pursuit of the nervous tension
of suspense while the horses are going round, or the
cards are being dealt. That is what feeds her craving,

not the gaining of gold, but the pulsating sense of risk
and the ecstasy of expectation.

Sometimes she takes her family during the summer
months to Boulogne, since
her husband can run over
there every now and
then, when he
can tear himself
from the calls
of business, and
his longing to
see his wife and
children will not
be gainsaid. But
does he find her play-
ing with their little ones on the sands? No, she
kisses them in the morning, and bids the nurse and
governess look carefully after them, and let them
enjoy themselves, and she sees no more of them that
day, unless, perhaps, when she returns to the hotel to
change her dress for the evening. Nevertheless, she
is intensely fond of her children, and if one should
have ever so slight an ailment she will be beside
herself with anxiety, send for the doctor two or three

times a day, and never leave the child's bedside, while she will lavish caresses upon her. But so long as the children are well and enjoying themselves on the sea-shore or in the gardens, she gives no heed to them during the day, her mind being absorbed by the question whether the nine will turn up at baccarat, or else whether the horse she has put her money on will be a winning one. It is not as exciting at Boulogne as at Monte Carlo, but it is a substitute, and it helps to keep up that feverish heat her nature needs to sustain it.

It is at Monte Carlo, however, that Mrs. Hazard really feels the full expansive joy of living. There she breathes excitement in the air, there she vents the full passion of her nature. The gaming tables at Monte Carlo appear to her the proper sphere of her life. The wonderful blue skies of the Riviera, the exquisite colour of the scenery, the beautiful exuberance of the flowers, the light and gaiety of the careless life, the variety of character and nationality that is lured to the sunny, seductive South—all this has little meaning for her except as an adjunct to the passionate pleasure of play. That draws her to Monte Carlo with the irresistible force of a magnet. When she first arrives she perceives that the sky is blue, but afterwards it might be yellow or red for all she would know from ocular observation. She knows that the gaming table is green ; but for the sky and the flowers she simply feels that they are beautiful, for she is intoxicated with the atmosphere of the place. All else but the tables is a kind of sensation in a dream—the tables alone are distinct and tangible. She is sensibly conscious that the rest exists, but she gives no thought to it. If, as she dresses herself in the morning, she looks out of the windows at the beautiful " blue deep " of the sky, it is only with a sense of gladness that another day of delicious excitement has dawned, and her thoughts are not concerned with the beauty of the earth and the sky in that land of sunshine and flowers, but with the chances of the table, the hazards of a "system," and the calculation of gains and losses.

And the sweet, peaceful moonlight resting over the place, cut by the dark shadows of the tall, straight palms and the eucalyptus-trees—does its gentle enchantment fall upon her soul after the excitements of the day ? No, it only whispers fresh awakenings of the gambling fever in her, as she mentally recapitulates all

the incidents of the day's play. But you must see her at
the tables! There she sits, a picturesque figure in the
midst of a motley, *bizarre* group of gamblers gathered
around the table, all eager and intense, most of them
maintaining a deliberate coolness, but all linked by a
common passion, the chance of gain. She was at the
doors of the Casino before noon, so as to secure her
seat, waiting amid a crowd which comprised some of
the gambling scum of Monte Carlo as well as illustrious
members of our own nobility. Then as she went in,
she made straight for the cloak-room, that she might
leave her wrap there and get a numbered ticket in
exchange. She was very eager about this, reading
the number excitedly, for Mrs. Hazard, like most
gamblers, is superstitious, and her present supersti-
tion is to place her stakes upon the numbers on the
roulette table corresponding with those on her cloak-
ticket. She feels that her luck to-day depends upon
this, just as on another day, perhaps, she will only
play when a certain *croupier* is officiating, believing
that he alone will bring her good fortune.

'Mrs. Hazard is a plunger, and she generally com-
mences operations with about fifty louis, so that her
winnings are proportionately large, and the stake is

substantial enough to make the excitement keen.
Once she has placed her pieces, nothing else has any
interest for her. She gives herself up, body and soul,
to the play. She knows nothing that goes on around
her. She takes no cognisance of the heartburnings,
the awful anxieties, or the intense pleasures that
may reveal themselves in the faces of other players.
She only notices the *croupier* and the table. Some
hopeless young man might have just lost the last
penny of his inheritance, and, unable to face ruin
might be leaving her side with despair on his face
and desolation in his heart, to seek the shameful
death of the suicide. Another might have squandered
a fortune he held in trust for others—perhaps helpless
children—and, having swerved from the path of
honesty, be doomed henceforth to a life of fraud and
degrading adventure. A wretched wife and mother
might have played her last stake, and thus lost her only
chance of redeeming her wrecked fortune and her
husband's credit, except at the price of her honour;
and these unhappy creatures might go their hopeless
ways, as others, sanguine or desperate, come and fill
their places; but Mrs. Hazard does not heed them.
They have no existence for her, though at any other

time her heart would bleed for them, and she would talk of them with deep womanly sympathy; now she only watches the numbers, and the little roulette ball, and her gold pieces.

All the time she is playing, people come and go, and crowd around—people of all kinds, and of every nationality, the Russian prince, the English "milord," the French *déclassée*, the German baron, the American millionaire, and the Italian tenor; but they might all be dummies for the notice she takes of them—and yet Mrs. Hazard is really fond of studying character and types. A famous and beautiful English actress stands perhaps just opposite to her, one who is proverbially lucky at the tables, and a crowd of onlookers gather round merely to watch her play, finding her infinitely more interesting when all her sensibilities are actually involved in the chances of the roulette, than when simulating the passions of a dramatic heroine. But though Mrs. Hazard is devoted to the pleasures of the theatre, and generally evinces the greatest interest in the personalities of the stage, she now remains quite unconcerned as to the proximity of this distinguished artist, whose very costume even would at any other time be an object of lively interest to her. While the gaming fever is upon her she is as one under a spell. She is as separate from her normal self as the opium-eater when the drug is working upon him.

But it is not only at the foreign gambling-tables that Mrs. Hazard finds vent for her speculative spirit. Unknown to her husband—who, by the way, is never permitted to know what sums she really wins or loses, for his steady-going business mind would be simply appalled at them—she watches the money market with a close and keen interest, and increases or diminishes her winnings at play by means of "flutters" on the Stock Exchange. On one occasion she nearly came to financial and domestic grief over these transactions, for she had been playing heavily, and an unexpected crisis found her at settling-day with a balance on the wrong side, greater than she was able to meet. She dared not go to her husband for help ; her luck at cards and on the racecourse was at the time persistently against her—she is an inveterate poker-player and backer of horses—and she was obliged to enlist the assistance of a handsome and wealthy young man of her acquaintance.

The confidential notes that passed between them, and

their unexplained private meetings, at length aroused
the suspicions of her husband, and their conjugal relations were for a time exceedingly strained, and I
doubt if these two have ever been quite as completely
trustful since. One or two lucky wins at Epsom, and
a few good nights at poker at friends' houses helped
to put her on her financial feet again, and the suspense
and excitement of this experience afforded intense
gratification to her gambler's spirit, but her husband
still feels, I think, that he was never told all the truth
about her confidential friendship with that seductive
young man. He must often wonder, too, how much
his wife really wins after those long sittings at the
card-tables, but as he always protests against her winning money from their friends, he must be conscious
that she keeps a good deal from his knowledge. At
all events, her bank pass-book is a sealed book to
him.

Mrs. Hazard is very keen about horse-racing. She
was bred in Yorkshire, and loves horses, and knows
the Stud-book almost by heart. She studies the
Racing Calendar, and follows the careers of the racers
with almost professional interest. A racecourse to
her is an Elysium, and among her social set are many

racing men, who give her "tips," while their wives invite her to accompany them to Sandown, Ascot, Kempton, and Epsom. Her husband takes no interest in this kind of thing, but he does not hinder her going, and she carefully omits to tell him the result of her day's betting.

And, after all, why should she tell him? It would only annoy him, and the excitement of the racing is over. She *must* bet and gamble, or life would be mere stagnation to her. The rearing of children, the display of the domestic affections, the shallow pleasures of Society, and the charms of culture, are not alone sufficient to satisfy the cravings of her nature, though they may be for many women. She can enjoy all these, but she must have in addition the intoxicating delights of chance and risk.

A SINGER—AND HER MOTHER

MISS EUTERPE DIATONE is a concert-singer of average talent and popularity, if you will take my word for it; but if you prefer to accept her own version of the matter, you will learn that her genius excites the jealousy of the entire musical profession, also that if the public could only get their rights and the complete satisfaction of their musical desires, they would never hear any woman sing other than Miss Euterpe Diatone. But the concert-agents and the *entrepreneurs* are, as she will tell you, so venal and obtuse, and so easily influenced by the jealousy of the other vocalists, who cotton to them, and bribe them, maybe—who knows? Anyhow, Miss Diatone can tell you of numbers of instances where other singers, of less ability and fame than herself, have had engagements which ought to have been offered to her; and she knows for a fact that the concert-givers cut their own throats by this policy, for friends of her own actually stayed away from those concerts, only because she was not engaged to sing.

Of course all this is conveyed in a tone of becoming modesty, and if you want confirmation of these blatant facts, you have but to ask Miss Diatone's mother, Madame Brown-Smith. Though, if you value my advice in any particular, you will be content with the daughter's statement, for Madame Brown-Smith has always much to say on the subject of her daughter; and beautiful as motherly devotion undoubtedly is, the professional enthusiasm of the vocalist's mother is apt to become a little oppressive. She is a veritable touter, regarding her daughter's voice as the commercial traveller looks upon the article of his trade, and "pushing" it accordingly. As you listen to her depreciating every vocalist in turn, and telling you how Euterpe was encored so many times at such a concert, whereas every other performer "finished without a hand," and how Euterpe was paid so much by such a publisher for singing a certain song, which is really such rubbish you have wondered how any one could have had the impertinence even to print it, you begin almost to wonder whether music is a "divine art" after all, and not a trade on a par with the selling of patent pills, soap, or grey shirtings. Truly the modern singer—and her mother—are terrible dis-illusioners.

When we think of all that music is, and all it means, its magic influence, its mighty power, and when we reflect that, through ts medium, as the rhythmic expression of all unspoken emotion, the singer or the player may soothe a single heart or move a multitude, awaken a soul to love or rouse a nation to patriotism, what can we say of the musician who, with this splendid gift of song, merely turns it to sordid account? And yet singers must live. That is the difficulty, for in these days art must suffer that artists may prosper.

Miss Diatone is not one to starve for the sake of art, nor is her mother one to let her, for Madame Brown-Smith has something personal to say in the matter. Did she not pay for her daughter's musical education out of the slender means her husband left her, and is it not fair that she should now enjoy the profits? But if her daughter studied the interests of art before popularity, the profits would be slight indeed. The fact is, it pays to sing commonplace songs, and the "royalty system" therefore provides an important portion of Miss Diatone's income. Moreover, Miss Diatone urges that she must sing what the public want to hear, and when she sings songs of the pretty-pretty order now in vogue, she is vociferously encored. Moreover, she receives a fee from the publishers of the song as well as from the concert-giver, whereas, if she were to sing any really artistic song, which, of course, she will pretend she would much prefer doing, her audience would, she believes, be sure to find it " above their heads " and would applaud her faintly, and the publishers would not find it worth while to give her a " royalty." The encore and the " royalty " seem indeed to be the goals of the modern concert-singers' ambition, and for these they will sell their artistic souls.

I do not know how it is, but as soon as the commercial aspect of the musical profession takes hold on the artist's life, it seems to narrow the soul, to prevent that true *camaraderie* which exists amongst all other artists than musicians, and to promote self-serving and jealousy. The struggle for existence in the musical world would too often appear to be opposed to magnanimity of mind and generosity of soul, for those who exhibit these qualities in their professional lives and in their art-work, are not, as a rule, among the prosperous. It is a small world, not the world of song, mark you, but the world of professional singers, and it is full of the littleness of small communities. Of course there are exceptions, but they only prove the rule.

Miss Diatone lives in the midst of this narrow world, with its warped personal interests and its jealousies, so opposed to the great world of art, which concerns itself with all humanity, but somehow she does not appear to realise that it is so. It has not yet been borne in upon her that the professionally musical community is not the centre of the universe, and that she is not the actual axis on which it turns. If such a knowledge were likely to come to her from any quarter, her mother would be in time to prevent it, for Madame Brown-Smith is her daughter's Barnum.

By the way, why she is called "Madame" Brown-Smith is a mystery, unless she considers that her daughter's *status* in the musical profession confers that distinction upon her as a right. There is often a good deal of mystification among musical artists on the subject of these prefixes. They would seem to regard the use of "Madame" as a sort of artistic degree, and many vocalists' mothers, adopting it in place of plain "Mrs.," appear to hold the title in trust for their daughters till they become too old to be styled "Miss" any longer.

Without any disrespect to mothers, for as a class I reverence them, I cannot help thinking how much pleasanter many vocalists I wot of would be if they had no mothers, or, rather, if they had not the mothers Providence has provided them withal. Now, Miss Euterpe Diatone would be quite a nice, companionable girl if it were not for that mother of hers. Of course, Diatone is only a pseudonym, adopted for professional purposes, but as Euterpe Brown-Smith—when her father was alive, and before her mother discovered that she was worth working as a means of income—she was unaffected, and quite popular among her school-friends, though somewhat inclining to personal vanity. Then she began to develop a singing voice of a quality beyond anything known in their social circle— Mr. Brown-Smith, by the way, travelled in something or other, and they lived at Peckham Rye— and the fullest musical resources of the local High School were called into requisition for the cultivation of her voice. Then she was sent to one of the academies of music, and became quite popular in the parlours of Peckham Rye and its vicinity. She was greatly in demand for penny readings, choral meetings, and social gatherings of all kinds; and, of course, with her went her mother, who shone with her accomplished daughter's reflected light, posed as the mother of the local *prima donna*, and made social capital out of the position.

Now Mrs. Brown-Smith, as she was then called, always had an eye to business, and, when her husband died, she bethought her of Euterpe's singing powers for support; so, by fanning her daughter's vanity in every particular, she encouraged her to study hard and win scholarships, until at the students' concert she attracted the notice of the professors, the press, and the concert-agents, and thereupon obtained her first professional engagement. She was a success with the public, and gradually her engagements became more frequent, and of a better and more lucrative class, until her name has now become familiar in concert-halls and drawing-rooms.

And now Miss Euterpe Diatone and her mother reside in a flat in the West-end, and give pleasant "afternoon teas," and are seen in many places honoured of Society. Miss Diatone is really a bright and engaging girl in her way, and if she wears her profession perpetually on her sleeve, so to speak, perhaps she finds it consistent with her advancement. But though Miss Diatone be welcome in many drawing-rooms, both socially and professionally, the same can hardly always be said of her mother; yet poor Euterpe is in the same case with Mary who had a little lamb, for wherever Miss Diatone goes her mother is sure to go.

If they happen to be on a visit at a country house, and a driving party is being made up for the young folk, while the elderly ladies are to stay at home, Madame Brown-Smith disconcerts everybody by asking where she is to sit, and, of course, she takes the very seat which had been set apart for the belle of the party. Then Miss Diatone has quietly to apologise for "poor Ma, who does so love the country," the while she is boiling with indignation that her mother has probably spoiled her chance of a future invitation. Yes, her mother is certainly a trial; but if Euterpe attempted to protest that people may invite a young singer without necessarily wanting her mother, Madame Brown-Smith would only accuse her of ingratitude and want of feeling. What then can she do? But they have frequent quarrels, owing to Miss Diatone's egotism and her mother's aggressiveness, which come into conflict.

The subject of young men is one perhaps most fruitful of quarrels. Euterpe Diatone, though she finds much pleasure and gratification in the applause of the public, and much profit to boot, is essentially a woman, and her vanity cries also for the satisfaction of personal conquest. Consequently there is no over-looking the fact that she is an unconscionable flirt of a kind that is very popular with men, while at the same time she always keeps an eye open to the chances of matrimony, and to the advancement of her popularity. She has a very taking manner with both men and women, but with men she will assume a sauciness that leads them to suppose they may

o

be familiar. Then she will at once stand on her dignity, and command their personal respect, af er which she will relapse again, and completely puzzle them.

By this means she keeps her admirers at beck and call, and they all agree that she is "as clever as she knows how"—what odious expressions they do use nowadays !—but that "you have to mind your P's and Q's with her," for she puts out her bristles of propriety at the least alarm. Still they do not propose marriage, and that is a subject of perennial annoyance to her. But perhaps Madame Brown-Smith may be in some measure accountable for this lapse of connubial courtesy on the part of Miss Diatone's admirers. To tell the truth, she has an unmistakable way of intimating that any one who married Euterpe would find to his cost that mother and daughter were inseparable ; though I cannot help thinking, from my personal observation of the young vocalist herself, that after marriage she would take an entirely different view of the matter from her mother. In the meanwhile, she realises with undisguised irritation that this mother of hers is spoiling all her matrimonial chances in her enthusiastic endeavours to further her daughter's professional interests, and perhaps, in a greater degree, her own comforts.

It must not be supposed that Euterpe is not fond of her mother, or that she does not pay her sufficient attention ; but she has acquired a habit of egotism, perhaps from the practice of constantly standing alone upon the platform, and facing the public on her own merits. When, therefore, Madame Brown-Smith's idea of her own importance increases with her daughter's professional and social status, and she monopolises the conversation with "*my* daughter" this, and "*my* daughter" that, and "*my* daughter" the other, Euterpe feels that she could create so much more favourable an impression concerning her own doings with the personal persuasion of her "I." As the Americans would say, she wants "to run her own show." And what concert-agent, what composer, what publisher, or even what conscientious critic, would not be more inclined to listen favourably to the autobiographical details of a fair and winning egotist, with all her charm of personality, than to the obvious advertising and touting of the young artist's aggressive mother? If Miss Euterpe Diatone makes herself amiable to us with an eye to business—knowing us to be in a position to assist her professionally, we amiably fall in with her views because, though one eye be to business, the other is to ourselves, and both are pretty. We are only men, after all. But with the mother, it is quite another thing. We respect her maternal solicitude and her business assiduity, but she is a bore—brutal though it sound to say so. Moreover, without her for show-woman I verily believe Euterpe Diatone would have been a truer artist and a nicer woman.

THE "DEAREST FRIEND"

A̠MONG women, I venture to think, friendship is
not temperamental, it is an accomplishment; and, at
the risk of bringing down upon my devoted head an
avalanche of feminine contradiction, I make bold to
say that real friendship, as understood by men, is rare
between women, though nearly every woman cherishes
a " dearest friend."

A woman's "dearest friend" is her familiar gossip,
her partisan, but seldom, if ever, the companion of her
soul, the true confidante of her inner self. Of course,
both she and her "dearest friend" would indignantly
repudiate this assertion, and vow that they severally tell
each other *everything*, that their confidence is mutual
and complete; but then dissimulation is so inherent in
women that they are not aware of it. They are not
analysing creatures as a rule, and they would as soon
admit their natural dissimulation, or their incapacity

for friendship with their own sex, from a man's point of view, as any of us would own to lacking a sense of humour, or being no connoisseurs in matters of art.

I believe that men can teach women friendship. though, perhaps, not until they have learnt the great lesson of love, for which they have a natural intuition. Then, women may be the friends of men, and very true and enduring friends too; but between woman and woman I doubt, as a rule, whether you would find the same kind of friendship as between man and man, or even as between man and woman, for women seldom trust each other entirely—of course, always taking into consideration the necessary proof of exceptions. But of "dearest friends" there is no lack—indeed some women occupy this position in a kind of wholesale way. They make "dearest friendship" the business of their lives, and prosecute it in quite a professional fashion; and, of course, those who are "dearest friends" to a large *clientèle* become obviously better and more comprehensive gossips.

Mrs. Meanwell is one of these; she is a general favourite, and carries with her an amiability as alluring as it is indiscriminate and universal. As a "dearest friend," therefore, she is in constant and general

demand, and consequently she is a veritable Pantech-
nicon of personal gossip. This vocation has been hers
since her earliest schooldays, when she was the
recipient of all the other little girls' confidences in
rotation, and, though uniformly cheery and good-
tempered, she was often the cause of heart-burning
in others. For, how could she be expected to respect
the secrets of her quondam friends when they had
quarrelled with her " dearest friend " of the moment?

Some people mysteriously inspire confidences, and
Mrs. Meanwell has always done so, and even more
now that she is a woman-of the-world than when she
was an unsophisticated school-girl. She has an amazing
gift of dissimulation, which would be invaluable to an
actress or a diplomatist, but which is of immense aid
in cultivating that reputation for sympathy which is
essential to the vocation of a "dearest friend." She
is able absolutely to absorb herself—to all outward
appearance—in conversation with the person who is
her companion for the time being, to seem to be
interested in nothing else in the world beyond the
topic of their talk, while all the time, perhaps, she is
really calculating the favourable impression she has
made upon the other person, and deciding how

uncongenial that other is to her. But her stock of gossip and her range of personal experience have increased the while, as her sympathetic influence has widened. She has prepared the way to be "dearest friend" to her recent companion, if she chose, and though she may have no desire for this, she is content with the sense of her power.

I have often watched Mrs. Meanwell with infinite curiosity and amusement, and seen her, within brief periods, receiving the voluminous confidences of two women I knew to be jealous foes, and I have wondered how she was able to maintain such intimate and seemingly affectionate relations with both But the secret lies in her pliable temperament, which she can temporarily assimilate to the idiosyncrasies of any person with whom she comes in contact. I have seen her apparently interested by men and women from

whose tedious society I would commit almost any enor-
mity to escape, and, I must say, from a philanthropic
point of view, I have admired Mrs. Meanwell for this
comprehensive amiability which could rescue these
people from the awful consequences of their own boredom. I have admired it in the same way that I admire
women who nurse the sick and solace the afflicted.
She is a kind of Florence Nightingale among the dull
and the bored, and a beautiful beneficence is hers—
mentally cheering those who through their own inherent dulness cannot possibly cheer themselves. But,
just as you hear hospital nurses and workers in the
slums say they actually love their work, so does Mrs.
Meanwell really find amusement even among the bores.
She is, of course, fond of hearing herself talk—who is
not that has anything to say ?—and she certainly glories
in extending her popularity.

It will be seen, therefore, that Mrs. Meanwell is
naturally fitted to fill the position of " dearest friend "
to all kinds and conditions of women, and, certainly,
her experience has been as varied as are her qualifica-
tions. Therefore, it could hardly be expected that she
would confine her sympathetic offices to one friend,
or be content with a single stock of confidences. At

the same time she is an enthusiastic partisan, and if any of her "dearest friends" be involved in any social squabbles, matrimonial troubles, or financial difficulties, she is on the warpath at once. She is like an Indian scout, and carries intelligence from camp to camp. Mrs. Meanwell has codes of loyalty of her own, and she is her own arbiter in the matter, women being proverbially unable to bind themselves arbitrarily to one code as men must do. For that reason we never talk of a woman of honour as we talk of a man of honour; it would be too unfair. Women have quite enough restrictions and responsibilities to bear without having to trouble themselves with an exacting code of loyalty towards each other. So a little elasticity in this matter is, perhaps, excusable— at all events, since feminine custom stales its infinite variety.

However, I daresay—in fact I feel sure—that Mrs. Meanwell is as loyal to her "dearest friends" as they are to her; and if mischief be sometimes made between them by the too officious repetition of some innocently-betrayed confidence, it is the fault of the person who made the mischief, not of Mrs. Meanwell, who never intended what she said to be told again.

And, of course, it has been entirely distorted in the telling. Is it likely that *she*, her dearest friend's " dearest friend," would tell anything told to her in confidence, if she thought it would be repeated? Not that Mrs. Meanwell received it originally as a confidence; she thought other people knew it too, and after all it was such a good story, and if it sounded rather unkind in the repetition, *she* never told it in that spirit. Had not her friend laughed herself when she told it to her originally? But some people have no tact, and never know when, where, or to whom a personal story may be told without offence. So Mrs. Meanwell was not really responsible for the ill-timed and unwarranted repetition, and to say she was disloyal is most unkind and unwomanly.

Who could resist such reasoning? Who could continue to regard Mrs. Meanwell other than as a " dearest friend " after such an unanswerable defence? Anyhow, the intermediary mischief-maker " it was who died," or rather who fell into disfavour, and she, after all, was absolutely innocent in the matter, and acted in perfect good faith, for she merely wished to warn her friend against being too confidential with a woman who gossiped about other people's affairs. Mrs.

Meanwell a gossip! What next, I should like to know? How these "dearest friends" love one another.

Mrs. Meanwell fights her friends' battles with the weapons of chaff and ridicule, and after her victories she generally manages to secure peace. That is one of the secrets of her success as a "dearest friend." The friend who, in times of trouble or quarrel, enlists the help or advocacy of Mrs. Meanwell, feels as sure of everything being put right as the litigant when he has secured the legal services of a George Lewis.

But it is not only in times of tribulation or difficulty that Mrs. Meanwell acts the "dearest friend" in very earnest. If an engagement be announced in her social circle she is the one to keep all her friends posted up in all the details, how long the affair has been in progress, when he first spoke out, what he said, what are the mundane prospects of the young couple, what arrangements have been made for the wedding, and last, but not least, the component parts of her trousseau. All these details have been confided to Mrs. Meanwell in her capacity as "dearest friend" of somebody very nearly connected with the bride or bridegroom. It is indeed a noteworthy coincidence that

when any interesting event is on the *tapis*, especially
a wedding, an engagement or a jilting, a good romantic
scandal, or a sensational illness, Mrs. Meanwell always
happens to be on terms of closest friendship with
somebody connected with it, so that she can ever
be relied on for the very latest and most accurate
information. She never minds how much trouble she
takes on these occasions to gain this information or
to give counsel when called upon. She has, by the
way, a reputation for practical wisdom in all things,
which has grown out of some occasional happy random hits in the way of advice on mundane matters,
the result of a clear wit that dominates the sentiment
in her nature, and thus enables her to keep her
"dearest friendships" well under control and to the
purpose.

Mrs. Meanwell's friends, it will be seen, consult
her on many things, but, perhaps, it is on the subject
of dress that she is at her best and strongest. She
has a veritable genius for costume, and has won many
a friend with the turn of a hat, the cut of a bodice,
the fall of a flounce, the hang of a skirt, or the
harmonious hues of an evening-gown. In matters
of clothes she has the critical eye of a Ruskin,

combined with the constructive imagination of a Worth, and, consequently, she is simply invaluable as an adviser to her friends, for that they shall dress well is a *sine quâ non* if they wish to retain her friendship.

Of course, this is not put in so many words, but it is a kind of tacit understanding, and half the confidences that pass between Mrs. Meanwell and her "dearest friends" bear on the absorbing topic of costume. She recognises it as an important social factor—and so do all the husbands and fathers when the dressmakers', drapers', and milliners' bills come in. But Mrs. Meanwell's friends, especially her "dearest" ones, have appointed her the arbiter of taste in costume, and, unfortunately for their husbands' pockets, her ruling is governed by a superb optimism, which, as the dictionary defines, is "the doctrine that everything is ordered for the best"—and, of course, the best has to be paid for. Economy is, in Mrs. Meanwell's opinion, a revolt against good taste, and her friends are easily persuaded by her superior logic, and those picturesque proofs of her judgment which their dressmakers turn out.

From the husband's point of view, however, there is

something to be said. Mrs. Meanwell, as "dearest friend," is an expensive luxury for the wife. But then, after all, perhaps, a female "dearest friend" is safer than a male one, and, if there be also a male one, she acts as a sort of safety-valve to let off those little romantic confidences which might not amuse the husband, yet which might possibly lead eventually to complications if suppressed in the wife's bosom, or entrusted to the loyal keeping of the male "dearest friend."

Therefore, Mrs. Meanwell conquers the economic considerations of the husbands, and remains the " dearest friend " of the wives, because of her approved worldly wisdom. And, after all, if they be a little extravagant, their wives look ever so much better when Mrs. Meanwell advises their costumes. And — well, it is very pleasant to have a charming little woman like Mrs. Meanwell coming frequently to the house, and staying there.

A "FIN-DE-SIÈCLE" WOMAN

THE habit of credulity is one of my peculiarities; some people indeed regard it as a fatal weakness, especially when it leads me to place implicit faith in women. Nevertheless I cannot bring myself to take Mrs. Reuben Neuralys quite seriously in all her social and psychical vagaries.

Every period grafts some special types of woman on to the Eternal Feminine, and Mrs. Neuralys represents quite a special type of the present. She is a very complex and not easily comprehended creature, and since it has lately become the fashion to describe anything that seems to elude ordinary classification as *fin de siècle*, I suppose I must regard Mrs. Neuralys as a *fin-de-siècle* woman. Certainly she has no counterpart in the pages of Jane Austen or Miss Mitford, and if we would find any approach to her prototype in fiction, we must look to the works of the later " realists." She

is perfectly conscious of this; in fact, she studies that
it shall be so, and acts up to it with picturesque effect.
And "there's the rub." One is constantly led to
suspect, by some little unconscious incongruous touch
of naturalism, that she is only acting the part of the
Emancipated Woman, that she is only playing at what
she has read and talked about, that after all there is
an artificial ring in this advanced development of
womanhood, as represented by Mrs. Neuralys.

Not that I discredit in any way the advancing condition of women, the greater freedom, mental, moral
and social, that they are gradually and justly assuming
as their right. But I always find that they take an
exaggerated view of their emancipation ; to prove their
independence they begin to shatter idols and scoff at
sacred things, after the manner of all revolutionists.
Yet though they consider their emancipation demands
that they shall at least affect to regard children as
intolerable nuisances and husbands as merely useful
appendages to their own lives and quite irrelevant to
their romances, only let a child of theirs be ill, or
a lover give cause for jealousy, and it is the uneman-
cipated, the real woman that will reveal herself in all
her elemental femininity.

P

I cannot say that Mrs. Neuralys belongs to the strong-minded sections of the Emancipated Sisterhood; she stumps no platforms and professes no mission; she sets herself no philanthropic task; she has adopted no vocation, unless it be that of living so as to best please Mrs. Reuben Neuralys. She cultivates a kind of world-weariness, and professes to be hopelessly oppressed by custom. She is bored by everything in which her foremothers were wont to take pleasure. The ruling passion of her life is novelty of sensation, and in seeking this she is utterly without conscience. No considera-tion of conventionality can restrain her in the pursuit of a new experience in emotion; no respect for tradition has weight with her to restrict any experiment in sentiment or sensibility. Anything that produces new psychical or sensuous effects upon her is welcomed, irrespective of Mrs. Grundy, the Ten Commandments, or Mrs. Lynn Linton. Whether it be a new religion, a new social environment, a new specific for neuralgia, to which she is of course a martyr, a new personality to love and be loved by, a new artistic cult, she will make for it with unbridled eagerness, no matter what social or other susceptibility she may shock in the accomplishment. I believe that she really enjoys the

sense of novelty, though I shrewdly suspect that she
affects many fancies and pretends many enthusiasms merely because she thinks that not to do so would be "conventional."

This word "conventional" is the bogie of her life, she is so afraid of it that she will run into any extravagance to escape its application. It is her own pet term of contempt— that and "sub-

urban." I believe she herself would rather be called

improper than suburban. To her mind, conscious, of course, of its own innocence, there might be something piquant in being thought improper; it might lead to new experiences of other people's real characters, shed side-lights on the world of men and women, and pluck for her the heart of many mysteries. For this reason she affects exceptional freedom of speech and licence of subject, and she expresses no anger, or only smiles, whenever mischievous persons couple her name with that of any man who may be openly admiring her at the moment, and whose escort to places of public resort she may constantly accept,— for of course, being an emancipated woman, it would be altogether too "suburban" to be seen about with her husband. Indeed she appears to deem it a point of honour, and an obligation due to the end of the century, to let it be clearly understood that her husband bores her, and that no sympathy of any kind exists between them. And certain of her friends, and I am told many wives of most affectionate disposition, con- sider that no self-respecting husband outside Peck- ham Rye and its like would wish it otherwise.

But, you may ask, what induced a woman like Mrs. Neuralys to marry at all, leastways this husband who bores her so? Might you not ask the same question about nine wives out of ten? Does any girl ever know exactly why she marries? Does she ever know really whether she is in love till after marriage? Is it not illusion in most cases—the love of a girl for a man? I do not think Mrs. Neuralys was ever really in love with Reuben, but she married him out of curiosity. I am betraying no confidence in saying this, for she herself has stated it frequently and openly, and I think she is rather proud of it. Certainly, the fact is characteristic of her, and in this wise.

Aline Aubyn, as she was then, was decidedly of a religious habit, but it was the mystery of religion that attracted her, while its shows appealed to her sensuous nature? To her it meant no spiritual communion, no divine faith, but the sounds of the organ and the choir and the church-bells caused her unspeakable emotions. She enjoyed the *sense* of the church with its stained-glass windows and its mediæval architecture and the devotional attitude of the congregation. When therefore her parents took her abroad and she visited many cathedrals, the vestments of the priests, the scent of the incense, the pretty acolytes, the mass-music and the general colour and picturesqueness, quickly converted her to the Church of Rome. The novelty of her conversion delighted her for a time, and she was assiduous in her attendances at chapel. But novelties have a way of losing their freshness, and, as I have said, Aline was not spiritually religious. Therefore when she met Reuben Neuralys, her interest took another turn, for he was the first Jew she had ever encountered. She had read and heard much of the Jews and their wonderful history, of their persecutions and their ancient rites, and to her the very name of Jew meant mystery. Reuben therefore appealed to her imagination, and exercised for the time being an extraordinary fascination over her. His manners were at all times charming, the bent of his mind distinctly idealistic, and his nature emotional. Aline's sensuousness and personal charms attracted him, though, in his idealistic way, he deceived himself into thinking the attraction was dominated by her spirituality. He loved her, and she fancied that being fascinated at the novelty of being loved by a member of a race she could not dissociate from mystery and mysticism was being in love. So they became engaged, and probably never would have married, but the parents on both sides made such strenuous opposition to the marriage, on the score of difference in religion, that the situation presented to Aline a romantically dramatic colour of irresistible and obstinate charm. There was one drawback however. The Registry office was so ugly, the ceremonial seemed so bare and common. It was a novelty to Aline certainly; but it was all unbeauti- ful, unbridal, and she hated it.

It did not take long to prove to Mr. and Mrs. Neuralys that they were temperamentally ill-suited to one another. Her illusions as to his ancient race had worn off, and she found him similar in manner and habit to any other ordinary young English gentle- man of University education and a comfortable worldly position for which others had worked. But perhaps he was more full of ideals than most young men of the day, and some of these ideals she proved im- practicable for him, notably that concerning the absolute union of a man and woman in love. She was disappointed in his Judaism, which had nothing mysterious or sensuous in it, and she seemed gradually to display personal indifference towards him, because he loved her uxoriously, and en- tertained patriarchal views with regard to conjugal life. She by no means falls in with these views, on the contrary she has asserted her individual liberty at all points, and though she was never one of those women who must love to live, she has ever held the opinion that for a woman to be interesting she must always be adored by more than her husband. She says that the adoration of a lover preserves her youth, and as she loves herself too much to fall really in love, and expresses only a kind of sympathetic scorn for those women who love "not wisely but too well," it may be supposed that she is still on the right side of the marriage contract. Anyhow her husband has faith in her to this extent, for it is a kind of racial instinct with Jews to believe in the purity of their wives, and though Reuben Neuralys has individually ceased to observe the ancient ceremonials of his creed his racial feelings continue very strong. So he has never a fear of the Divorce Court, although he has realised his wife's sensuous craze for novelty simply because it is novelty, and discovered that she is pretending to be always in love, first with one man who has superficially inducted her into the mysteries of Esoteric Buddhism, then with another who has engaged her fancy with Ibsen, Schopenhauer and the Fabian Essays, and anon with a third who has persuaded her that all pleasure is Pagan, and that pure Hedonism can alone make the world beautiful. As it is only in the nature of things that the cause of each of these successive loves should prepare some distrust of the next, Reuben Neuralys, knowing his wife's temperament, regards these as extra safeguards rather than as dangers. Moreover, since he has ceased to expect from her that complete companionship and passionate sympathy he had hitherto regarded, in his idealistic way, as the natural bonds of married life, he has accustomed himself to look for these elsewhere. And she more than suspects this—and does not care. "Poor fellow," she says, and laughs. She is a *fin-de-siècle* wife, you know.

Thus they live, these two, practically separate, though always meeting at dinner-time. He, practising little deceptions which she always suspects or detects but never exposes, for fear he should discontinue them and bore her instead; she, simulating occasional moods of sentiment and even affection, and dexterously playing upon the most sensitive chords of his nature, when she fancies it necessary to preserve her empire over him, and cozen him into accordance with her wishes. She is so absolute in her desire for power and ascendancy that she would battle hard to retain the admiration of even a husband, how ever little she might really value it. Nevertheless they go their separate ways pleasantly, and if they never talk of happiness, perhaps, under the circumstances, their unconventional but easy and casual philosophy of matrimony is preferable to the perpetual bickerings, or heart-breaking suppression of feelings, which so often mar the more domestic households.

But I fear I may be conveying an impression that Mrs. Neuralys is not all she should be, which would be unjust—to say the least of it. What can I say to correct any such impression? Let me catalogue her virtues.

However tastes may differ, no one can deny that she is piquantly pretty. Ask all the best photographers in London, ask at least one of our most artistic young painters. Look round his studio-walls, they will testify extensively to her facial charms. Then, how she dresses—why, Venus' herself might have dressed so, had she been born in the fashion. In her monetary dealings she is liberal to a fault, and, as her tradespeople and dressmakers, who all adore her, will tell you, the fault is always on the right side—

she never inquires the cost of anything. And so affable too, she frequently drinks afternoon-tea with her milliner, who is of course socially her equal. Indeed I am not certain that Mrs. Neuralys does not hanker after adopting some such profession herself, by way of a new experience, and, if she did, I am sure her bonnet-shop would be the most alluring boudoir in London. But, intellectually, she is really above this kind of thing. She has not read Schopenhauer and all the latest English and foreign "realists," and pessimistic critics for nothing. She is alive to every new "movement" in art, literature, religion or the drama, and as long as it is new and provocative of opposition from the advocates of the traditional, it will be sure of her ardent and aggressive partisanship. The very opposition will flatter her into thinking she is asserting her own individuality, for, of course, she forgets that she is only following a lead and running in a groove. Moreover she will think she is sincere in professing admiration for eccentric authors worshipped by experimental cliques, whereas if they were popular, and were accepted by the "plain man" of the *Times* and the *Nineteenth Century*, I doubt if she would concern herself with them, however good they might be. In everything her taste must be as unconventional as her daily life. She is so impressionable, she will tell you, so sensitive to all that is beautiful or *bizarre*.

At the same time Mrs. Neuralys unflinchingly seeks to know life in all its phases, however shocking to the ordinary "suburban" mind. She will go to a music-hall, a race-meeting or a Salvation Army service with equal alacrity, so long as her husband does not take her. He may make one of a *parti carré*, but alone he would bore her. She is a ravenous reader of newspapers, and to see her devouring some notorious divorce case in a "special edition" over her coffee and cigarette is to see the *fin-de-siècle* woman quite at home. She is a most assiduous theatre-goer, and is frequently met at the first performances of new plays, but she regards the modern drama in a very pessimistic light, and, for the moment, she may possibly affect to believe that its regeneration can only be brought about through the influence of a new Hottentot dramatist of pristine simplicity, about to be discovered by the very newest critic of the day. She is always most enthusiastic about matters of this kind, and ever alert for the latest.

But I wonder what Mrs. Neuralys will be like when she is old; whether, indeed, old age will be tolerable to her without any backbone of faith and domesticity. Can she always remain an Emancipated Woman, or, as the years pass, will the humanity that is in her cry out for something more tangible than the showy make-believe of her present life, something truer, something more sacred and beautiful? Who can tell?